CASE NURSE

When Karen Gregory arrives at Glen Hall to nurse the elderly matriarch of the Murrays, the desolate surroundings immediately dampen her spirits. Mrs Murray's sons are at odds with the housekeeper; and the younger one, Roy, introduces himself to Karen with a kiss! Then an injury which might not be accidental sends the older son, Duncan, to hospital; a situation that ultimately results in Karen being ordered to leave the Hall. But she's determined to help — and she's already fallen in love with one of the handsome brothers . . .

Books by Phyllis Mallett
in the Linford Romance Library:

LOVE IN PERIL
THE TURNING POINT
LOVE'S MASQUERADE
POOR LITTLE RICH GIRL
ISLE OF INTRIGUE
HOUSE OF FEAR
DEADLY INHERITANCE
THE HEART IS TORN
SINISTER ISLE OF LOVE
MISTRESS OF SEABROOK
HER SEARCHING HEART
TIDES OF LOVE
INTRIGUE IN ROME
DANGEROUS LOVE
IMPETUOUS NURSE
NURSE ON SKIS
PATIENT NURSE
MARRIED TO MEDICINE
DOCTOR'S DESTINY
EMERGENCY NURSE
DISTRICT NURSE
ROMANTIC DOCTOR
COUNTRY DOCTOR

PHYLLIS MALLETT

CASE NURSE

Complete and Unabridged

LINFORD
Leicester

First published in Great Britain in 1970

First Linford Edition
published 2019

A catalogue record for this book is available from the British Library.

ISBN 978–1–4448–4165–7

Published by
F. A. Thorpe (Publishing)
Anstey, Leicestershire

Set by Words & Graphics Ltd.
Anstey, Leicestershire
Printed and bound in Great Britain by
T. J. International Ltd., Padstow, Cornwall

This book is printed on acid-free paper

1

Karen Gregory decided it would take her a considerable time to settle down in Glen Hall, a sprawling stone mansion set in a desolate part of the Scottish Highlands some miles away from the town of Glen Tay. The massive house had overawed her at first sight, and she paused in her task of putting away her clothes in the cupboards of the high room to which she had been shown and went to the narrow window to peer out at the wild country that surrounded the estate. She was still trembling inside at the bleak reception she had received from the housekeeper, as if she were to blame that the local doctor had fetched in an English nurse for the mistress of the Hall instead of some local angel of mercy. But she was under control now, and her concerns were only for the patient. Old Mrs

Murray was still very seriously ill, and would need long and careful nursing if she were to be pulled through.

The dark furniture of the room, and all the dull wooden panelling, had a depressing effect upon her, and Karen sighed heavily as she went back to her unpacking. Even the thin rays of the late summer sun failed to cheer her, and she wondered if she had made a mistake in accepting this post. She sat down on the creaky bed, and grimaced when she discovered that it was hard and uncomfortable. No modern interior sprung mattress for her! But the whole house and its contents seemed ages old, and no-one seemed concerned that the entire place was going rapidly into the middle stages of decay.

A tap on the door aroused her, and she got quickly to her feet and went in answer, thrusting aside her foreboding. It didn't matter that she might not be happy here. Her duty was to her patient, as yet unseen, and her own personal feelings didn't enter into the case.

A tall, heavily built man stood in the corridor, a glowering expression upon his heavy but handsome face. He was very dark skinned, and his unruly black hair hung over his forehead. His teeth were startingly white as he showed them in a smile, and when he spoke his voice had a lilt to it that attracted her and sounded pleasing.

'You'll be Nurse Gregory,' he said. 'I'm Duncan Murray, the eldest son here. I'm sorry I wasn't able to get to the station to meet you personally, but I trust the alternative arrangements I made were satisfactory.'

'Yes thank you, Mr Murray,' Karen said slowly. 'I arrived safely. In fact I was so taken up with the scenery that I hardly noticed the distance.'

'Do you think you'll like it here?' he demanded.

'I'm sure I shall!' She nodded quickly. 'But I'm more concerned about my patient. I haven't seen Mrs Murray yet.'

'Hasn't that old hag Amena Lachlan

taken you in to see her yet?' He frowned, his brows drawing together, seeming to cling to his lower forehead in perilous fashion. 'I told her to take you to Mother as soon as you arrived.' He sighed heavily and shook his dark head. 'Have you settled in yet? Finished unpacking?'

'Just about!' She smiled, feeling a little easier at the sound of friendliness in his tones. 'I would like to see Mrs Murray now. I understand the doctor will be calling soon, and he'll give me all the details of the case, but it's imperative that I do see the patient as soon as possible and begin to familiarize myself with her condition.'

'You're enthusiastic about nursing then?'

'It's not mere enthusiasm,' Karen replied. 'There's much more to it than that.'

'Of course.' There was just the slightest trace of an accent in his tones, and she guessed he had received his education in England, and at a very good school. He sighed again, and made a small impatient gesture. 'I gave orders for you to be given the room next to my mother's! It's just dawned on me that I've even been disobeyed in that! Come along, Nurse, and I'll show you to my mother's room, and I'll have your clothes and everything else moved to a better room. This part of the house is the servants' quarters.'

Karen thought of the hard, lumpy mattress on the bed in the room, and nodded as she walked with him along the wide corridor. They turned a corner, and Karen saw immediately that they were entering a better part of the house. There was a thicker carpet on the floor and the panelling around the walls was of a lighter, more modern shade.

'I'm not going to have you treated as a mere servant,' Duncan Murray said firmly. 'You'll take your meals with us and be treated as a special guest.'

'Please, there's no need to go to those lengths,' Karen said. 'I'm here to do a job and I'll slip quietly into the routine of the house.'

'I would make you a special guest to spite Mrs Lachlan if I hadn't already decided that your position ought to be above that of a lackey,' he said severely, and Karen decided not to pursue the matter. He glanced at her as they reached the main staircase that spiralled up from the wide hall. 'Sorry,' he said briefly. 'I don't want you to get the wrong impression of this place, but there is a tug of war going on between me and the main servants. I'm referring to Mrs Lachlan and her husband Robert, who is the gardener. They're beginning to act as if they own the place, and I don't get along with them.' He paused and thrust out his bottom lip, his expression pensive for a moment. 'But don't let me drag you into the local situation. You'll have your work cut out nursing my mother.'

'I understand that she's been very ill,' Karen said gently.

'We almost lost her, and would have done so but for Doctor Sloan. He did magnificently! And when he suggested a nurse to help out I immediately took his advice. He engaged you?'

'He must have contacted the bureau on whose books I am!'

'You look competent!' His face showed approval. 'I'm sure you'll have no problems here, except loneliness, probably. But we'll do all we can to make your stay a happy one.'

'Thank you!' Karen paused as he opened a door, and she followed him into the large bedroom, her eyes going immediately to the big, old-fashioned four poster bed by the tall windows. She saw a small figure lying under the bedclothes, and one glance at the immobile features of the sick woman informed her of the seriousness of the patient's condition.

'She had a stroke,' Duncan Murray said softly, pausing on the threshold with Karen at his side. 'She partially recovered from that and got up, but caught pneumonia and almost slipped away from us. I hope she'll take to you because she's a strange old lady, and she would make your life hell if she didn't take a fancy to you.'

'I'll do my best in any situation,' Karen said quietly, and he looked at her, nodding his approval.

'Don't stand any nonsense from any of the staff,' he said in low tones. 'Just let me know if they try to give you any trouble.'

Karen did not reply, but approached the bed, her eyes studying the wan features of the woman lying there. She had been told that Mrs Murray was sixty-seven, but her first glance at the pale features made her want to add ten years to her judgment. She saw the eyes flicker open, and paused as she was surveyed by them. Duncan Murray moved up beside her, and Karen felt oddly comforted by his presence.

'How are you feeling now, Mother?' he demanded, and didn't wait for a reply. 'This is Nurse Gregory. She's just arrived. I want you to give her a fair chance. She's going to do all she can to help you.'

Mrs Murray nodded slightly. Her gaze did not leave Karen's face. Her lips moved as if she would speak, but she shook her head slowly and closed her eyes. Karen glanced at Duncan Murray, and he smiled reassuringly as he caught her eye. He went closer to the bedside and reached out a large hand to touch his mother's thin arm.

'Mother, I want you to give Nurse Gregory a fair chance. She will have a lot to put up with from Amena! Remember that she is here to help you, and Doctor Sloan sent for her. You trust his judgment, don't you?'

Mrs Murray opened her eyes and stared at Karen again. This time there was a little warmth in her eyes. She moistened her lips and spoke in quavering tones.

'I hope you will be able to enjoy your stay in this house, Nurse. There is only one thing I ask of you.'

'Anything, Mrs Murray,' Karen said instantly.

'Don't wear your uniform.'

'All right!' Karen nodded. 'That's easily arranged.' She moved closer and tugged the bedclothes gently, an automatic gesture that was not lost on Duncan Murray. He moved back a bit, nodding to himself. 'Is there anything I can get you, Mrs Murray?'

'Not right now. Doctor Sloan will be coming in later, and he'll want to have a talk with you.' The sick woman sighed deeply and relaxed a little. 'You'll take charge of all medicines, won't you?'

'Of course!' Karen glanced at the little table beside the bed, on which stood several bottles and phials. 'You don't need those in here. I shall keep them in my room.'

'Which will be next door,' Duncan Murray said firmly. 'See, Nurse, there's a connecting door so you won't have to use the corridor at night. It'll be much simpler for you next door than in the room Amena selected for you.' He reached out and took hold of his mother's hand, and she smiled faintly as he bent to kiss her forehead. His face softened for a moment, and Karen, watching closely, was pleased to see his sudden tenderness. He seemed a very dour man until he smiled, but such a simple action changed his whole manner completely. 'If there's nothing you want now, Mother, I'll show Nurse Gregory around the house so she'll know where she is.'

'I shall be all right until the doctor comes,' Mrs Murray said faintly, and closed her eyes and seemed to relax into sudden sleep.

'Come along, Nurse,' he said, and led the way from the room.

Karen was interested in the old house, and Duncan Murray was pleased to show her around. There were a great number of rooms on three floors, and she lost count of them before they had covered half the area. But she saw that the majority of the rooms were neglected and decaying. Woodwork was rotting away, and old paint was peeling from the dingy surfaces. But evidently Duncan Murray didn't see any of this, and Karen found herself wondering why he deluded himself. He had the air of a man showing around a party of visitors to a stately home, and she wondered if familiarity had blinded him to the true state of affairs in his home.

When they returned to the ground floor Karen began to tense, for she knew a battle would commence when they faced the old housekeeper. It seemed to her that a struggle had existed here in the house long before her arrival, but she would be used as a pawn in it, to further the course of the strife.

'We'll get this business of your room sorted out now,' Duncan Murray said, and he glowered as he crossed the wide, stone-paved hall to the large kitchen. Karen went with him, and she could not prevent a wave of repugnance striking through her as she prepared for the unpleasantness. She certainly hadn't taken a liking to the housekeeper, who had made her attitudes quite plain upon Karen's arrival.

Amena Lachlan, the housekeeper,

was in the kitchen when they entered, and there was another, much older woman with her, both seated at the huge wooden table and drinking tea. Their conversation faded instantly and the housekeeper stared suspiciously at Karen.

'Nurse Gregory, I want you to meet Ilka Ferguson,' Murray said, advancing to the table and confronting the woman Karen hadn't seen before. 'She's my mother's cousin, and has been living here for years.'

Miss Ferguson held out a hand, and Karen was pleased to take it. She found herself regarded by a pair of pale blue eyes endowed with a sharpness that seemed to strike right through Karen. But a smile of welcome came to the wrinkled face.

'I'm glad you're here, Nurse. Mrs Murray does need special nursing now. I hope you'll be able to do much for her.'

'Thank you. I'm certain we'll have her on her feet again in no time.'

'Amena, why the devil did you put Nurse Gregory in the servants' quarters? I told you distinctly that she was to occupy the room next to my mother in order to be on hand if needed. This is the last time I'm going to tell you. Disobey my orders again and I shall have to think seriously about finding another housekeeper.'

'That's something you can't do!' Amena Lachlan stared at him with something like triumph showing in her dark eyes. 'My position here is secure until the day I die.'

'If you want me to put that to the test then I'll gladly oblige,' Duncan Murray said pleasantly, but there was a touch of steel in the undercurrents of his voice. 'Where's Deidre? I want Nurse Gregory's clothes moved to that room next to my mother's immediately.'

'It's the maid's half day,' Miss Ferguson said. 'But I'll help you move your things, Nurse.'

'I'll be able to manage,' Karen said with a smile. 'But thank you for offering. I'd better make the change now, before I start my duties.'

'I'll go up to the room to see that everything is ready for you,' Duncan Murray said. He glared at the glowering housekeeper. 'There's going to be trouble if that room hasn't been cleaned, I can tell you.'

Amena Lachlan pulled a face, and Karen suppressed a sigh as she followed Murray from the kitchen. He paused in the hall and turned to face her, shaking his head as he did so.

'I don't know what this place is coming to,' he said ruefully. 'I must apologize for this unnecessary trouble. I left strict orders this morning about your reception. But my father is to blame for this situation. The will he left has caused a lot of trouble.'

Karen said nothing, and they ascended the stairs in silence. But she could not help feeling uncomfortable, although her part in this situation was quite plain. She was here to take care of an invalid, and that was simple enough. She knew where her duty lay, and nothing beyond that would be able to affect her.

They reached the first landing, and then the doorbell rang. Murray paused and glanced at Karen.

'That's probably Doctor Sloan,' he said. 'Let's wait a moment to find out, shall we? You'll want to see him, of course.'

Karen nodded, and they waited on the stairs. Beneath them the short, stout figure of Amena Lachlan appeared from the kitchen, and the woman was grumbling as she scurried towards the front door. A moment later the door creaked open and the housekeeper stepped back a pace as a tall man entered. The sound of their voices came up the stairs, although Karen couldn't make out what was being said.

'That's Doctor Sloan,' Duncan Murray said. 'I'm glad he's here. You'll be able to have a long talk with him about Mother. I'll attend to your room while you're busy with the doctor.'

Karen nodded, and watched the

figure of the doctor as the man crossed the hall to the foot of the stairs. She had been expecting an old man, and didn't know why, but Doctor Sloan was tall and fair-haired, not more than thirty, and he seemed an athletic figure. He came up the stairs two at a time, and when he reached the landing he became aware of their presence, and paused and looked at them.'

'Good afternoon, Duncan,' he said in low tones. 'How is your mother today?'

'About the same, Doctor,' Murray replied. He glanced at Karen. 'This is Nurse Gregory. She's just arrived.'

'How do you do, Nurse?' Phelan Sloan held out his hand, and Karen was pleased to grasp it. The atmosphere of the house, combined with the unfriendly welcome she had received from the housekeeper, made her feel dismayed, but here was a powerful ally, someone from the world of medicine, and this she understood completely. 'I trust you had a good trip from London. Is this your first time in Scotland?'

'How do you do, Doctor?' she replied happily. 'I had a nice trip, thank you, and it is my first time in Scotland.'

'I hope you won't find it too lonely here,' he commented. 'Have you met Mrs Murray yet?'

'We were in to see Mother some time ago,' Duncan Murray said. 'I think they'll get along well together.'

'Well that's good news.' Phelan Sloan's blue eyes sparkled. 'I don't mind telling you, Nurse, that I've been worried about your coming. Mrs Murray is dead set against having a nurse in the house, and it took me a considerable amount of persuasion to talk her around. However you're here now, and in a week or two we should see a great deal of difference in Mrs Murray's condition. Let's go and see her now, shall we?'

Karen nodded, and followed him up the rest of the stairs. Duncan Murray left them at the door of his mother's room, pausing to remark to Karen that he would be attending to her room if she needed him, and Doctor Sloan opened the door of the sick room and they entered.

Mrs Murray was not asleep, but she did not rouse up a great deal at their presence. Sloan spoke to her in low tones, and examined her swiftly. After the examination he became more cheerful, and chatted with Karen in an effort to get Mrs Murray into a more receptive frame of mind. He gave Karen details of the treatment he wanted Mrs Murray to have, and by the time he was ready to depart the sick woman was looking more animated.

'I can safely leave you in Nurse Gregory's capable hands, Mrs Murray,' he said at length. 'She's a highly qualified nurse, and if you do everything she says then we'll soon have you out of that bed and getting around as of old. I'll give her instructions for handling you, and I'll call in daily as usual. But now I must be going, and in future I shall be looking for a lot of progress from you.'

'Thank you, Doctor.' Mrs Murray closed her eyes, and Sloan remained staring at her for a moment before shaking his head slowly and moving to the door, motioning for Karen to accompany him.

Out in the corridor the doctor paused, and he searched Karen's face for some moments before speaking.

'This is going to be a difficult case, Nurse, despite what I said in there,' he commented. 'Mrs Murray has lost the will to live. Her husband died a few months ago, and his death is directly responsible for her present condition. There's not much you'll be able to do for her apart from seeing she takes the medicine I have prescribed. But above all you must keep her cheerful and looking outward. Have you met Roy Murray yet?'

'Roy Murray?' Karen shook her head. 'Is he another son?'

'Yes, the younger. Duncan, whom you have met, is the nicer of the two, and very dependable. He takes care of the estate — what's left of it. But Roy gives his mother plenty of trouble. He's only twenty-seven, but one would have thought he'd have settled down by now.'

'There seems to be a lot of tension in this house,' Karen said uncertainly.

'You mean the housekeeper!' Doctor Sloan smiled. 'She's a strange old Highland lady, but I suspect her bark is worse than her bite. I don't think she'll make much trouble for you because she has Mrs Murray's interests at heart, and once she sees how you'll be helping Mrs Murray she'll come down on your side. She can't for the life of her see why I should have brought in an outsider when there are so many good Scottish nurses around, but it was a matter of convenience. I've used the bureau before, and I knew they could be relied upon to send someone fitting to the case.' He paused and smiled. 'I can see they haven't failed me this time, Nurse. I hope you'll be very happy here, and don't ever hesitate to contact me for anything you may need.'

'Thank you, Doctor, but I don't care about whether I shall be happy here or not. My only concern is for Mrs Murray, and you can rest assured that I'll see she gets nothing but the best attention.'

'Good. Thank you, Nurse. I shall be calling in from day to day, so you can expect to see a great deal of me. But now I'd better be on my way or I shall never get done today.'

Karen walked down the stairs with him, and he gave her some last minute instructions before departing. Then he opened the door and went off, and she closed the door and stood there for a few moments, thinking over what had been said. She began to revise her first opinions, and her dismay vanished when she realized that all she had to do was win over Amena Lachlan and the rest would be easy. There were no other problems in this house. Duncan Murray was most helpful, and being the eldest son his word would carry weight around the house. Karen was glad he was on her side, although his manner was a bit distant.

She jerked herself from her thoughts as the big door at her side was suddenly opened, and she looked up, startled slightly by the swift appearance of the tall, dark young man who came barging in. He pulled up short at the sight of her, and in that first instant Karen could guess that he was Roy Murray, because he looked so much like Duncan.

'Hello,' he said, and his tones were rich with the lilt of the Highlands. 'Who are you?' He paused. 'Don't tell me! You're the nurse! Well, well! You're a beauty, and no mistake. Doctor Sloan certainly knows his business. But I don't know what effect you'll have upon my mother. All I do know is that if I were ill and you came in to nurse me I'd recover quicker than if you performed a miracle.'

He crowded closer, and Karen gave ground, bewildered by his extrovert manner. Then she gasped, for he put his arms around her shoulders before she could realize what he was about, and then she was struggling in his arms and he was kissing her passionately!

2

The incident occurred in the space of a second or two, but it seemed like hours before Karen could break out of his grip. She was angry, her face red, and emotion was pumping through her breast. Surprise and shock took hold of her, and she stood facing him with shoulders heaving when he eventually released her and stepped back.

'How dare you!' Karen didn't know exactly what to say.

'Take it easy!' He was smiling again, his dark eyes agleam with pleasure and amusement. 'I always make it a habit to kiss a lovely girl whenever I get the chance. But what's in a kiss? There's no need to act as if I'd pulled the house down on top of you.'

'Roy!' Duncan Murray's voice cracked from the stairs, and Karen half turned to see the man coming down swiftly towards them.

'Hell!' Roy Murray tightened his lips. 'Here comes old spoil-sport! I suppose he's been making himself very useful around you, Nurse.'

Karen made no reply. She was too busy trying to regroup her scattered wits. Shock was vibrant in her mind, and she could feel the hot imprint of his kiss still upon her trembling lips. It had been a long time since she was last kissed! A picture of Nigel Chilton came to her mind. There was still a little pain in her heart over Nigel, and all that had finished three years ago! But she hadn't been kissed since, and the incident had upset her far more than she realized.

'Roy, what the devil are you playing at?' Duncan Murray demanded as he reached the foot of the stairs. 'This is Nurse Gregory, and she's not of the likes of the girls you know. If I catch you so much as looking twice at her in future I'll come down hard upon you.'

'Do you think you still can?' the younger man demanded, and his teeth glinted as he grinned. His dark eyes came in Karen's direction, and she felt her heart begin to pound despite herself. 'I'm sorry, Nurse! If I had known it would upset you I wouldn't have done it. But if more men went through life with my outlook then the world would be a far better place.'

'Leave her alone.' Duncan spoke harshly, and Karen was surprised by the anger in his voice. 'What do you want here?'

'What do I want?' A shadow crossed Roy Murray's face, and his lips thinned. He glanced towards Karen again, as if to say that this was none of her business and ought not to be discussed in her presence. Then he nodded slowly. 'I've come to see my mother!' he retorted. 'Have you any objections, Duncan?'

'None whatever, but you won't go barging in. Nurse Gregory is in charge of the case now, and you'll ask her when you can see Mother. There are some new rules in force in this house, Roy, and you'd better see to it that you obey them. There's been far too much unpleasantness in the past, and I won't stand for any more. Now behave yourself and act your age. One would have thought you could have grown out of these unfortunate habits, but I can see that time is never going to make any difference to you.'

'I'll take that as a compliment,' Roy Murray said, smiling, but his dark eyes were hard and proud. He glanced at Karen again, coolly, appraisingly, and she flushed as she met his gaze. 'When can I see my mother?' he demanded softly.

'I'll go up to her room immediately,' she replied. 'If you would care to wait outside the door I'll let you know if she is awake.'

For some reason Karen felt uncomfortable as she led the way up the stairs, and Duncan remained at the bottom, watching their progress with harsh gaze. Roy Murray kept at her side, and remained silent until they reached the first floor.

'Sorry if you took that little incident the wrong way,' he said when she paused outside the door of his mother's room. 'It wasn't intended to offend. I was surprised to see you in the house, and you looked so inviting. You'll know by now that I'm a weak character. Well I was certainly caught off guard when I saw you.' He grinned, and she told herself that he was startlingly handsome. She could still feel the tingling where his lips had pressed against hers, and a flush came to her cheeks again as she remembered the vital moment when he had held her in his strong arms.

'I'll see if your mother is awake,' she said softly. 'I won't keep you a minute.'

'Why aren't you in uniform?' he asked. 'I'm sure you'd make quite a picture.'

'Your mother has expressed a wish not to see me in uniform,' Karen replied, and she could not prevent a feeling of friendliness filling her towards this young man despite the way he had greeted her arrival. At least he was human! The thought crossed her mind and she smiled as she entered the sick room.

Mrs Murray was awake, and her dark eyes followed Karen's every movement. She nodded tiredly when Karen announced the arrival of her younger son, and Karen went to the door to admit him. She waited while Roy Murray crossed to the bed, and she was a little surprised by the degree of emotion he expressed when he spoke to his mother. No matter what troubles he gave her, he could not deny that he loved his mother! Karen tiptoed from the room, and she waited outside in the hall, her mind filled with conflicting thoughts. A host of new impressions had invaded her mind since her arrival, and she had not yet found the time to sort them. But she was certain she had run the gamut of every human emotion in the scale in the past two hours, and none had more impact upon her than that unexpected moment when she had been in Roy Murray's arms.

She went into the adjoining room and found that it was ready for her occupation. While waiting for Roy Murray to emerge from the sick room, she went along the corridor to the room the housekeeper had given her and began removing her clothes. Roy Murray appeared at the door of the adjoining room when she was almost finished with her changing over.

'Hello,' he said in some surprise. 'Moving out?'

'No, moving in!' Karen paused and smiled. 'I was put into the wrong room to start with.'

'Accidently?' He shook his head as he came into the room and sank down upon her bed, studying her lovely face with alert eyes. 'I'll wager it was some of Amena's doings! I know that old woman better than any. She doesn't want you in the house. If you hope to have any sort of a tolerable life here then you're going to have to win that housekeeper over to your side. Think you can manage it?'

'I greatly hope so! The less I have to worry about the situation in the house the more efforts I can devote to nursing your mother.'

'Then you'll find that I'm on your side,' he retorted. 'Tell me about yourself. Don't let me stop you in what you're doing, but tell me all about yourself. Where do you come from and what have you been doing with your life?'

'My story is very easily told,' she retorted, folding her clothes and putting them away. 'I'm a London girl, and I've spent most of my time since finishing my education just learning to be a nurse.'

'Have you worked in a hospital?' he demanded.

'Of course! Where else would I have received my training?'

'Well I don't know anything at all about nursing. You'll get on well with me if you can do anything for my mother. Doctor Sloan never tells me anything at all about my mother's condition. I never see him, so I have to rely upon Duncan's reports. No doubt you've guessed that Duncan and I don't hit it off very well. He's always been the responsible one. Being the elder of the two, he's seen his duty and always done it. I've never given a damn about this pile of rotting stone, but I do love my mother, and I want her to get better. I'm prepared to do anything to see that come about, so at anytime you feel my mother isn't getting the best then you let me know.'

'I assure you that I have your mother's interests at heart, and nothing will be too much trouble during the course of nursing her.'

'I know that!' He smiled. 'You didn't have to tell me. I summed you up the moment I got you in my arms. You're the better type of nurse, and Doctor Sloan did the right thing when he ignored Amena's advice and sent to London for you.' He laughed slowly. 'I have to tell you. Amena's widowed daughter is some sort of a nurse, and the old fool wanted her let loose in this house to take care of my mother.'

So that was the reason for the old housekeeper's animosity! Karen nodded to herself. That fact would enable her to plan her approach to the old woman's sympathy, but it was a harsh fact, and it would be a difficult feat to overcome the old woman's natural loyalties and make an unreserved friend of her. The daughter would always be an obstacle.

'But don't you worry about a thing,' Roy Murray went on. 'If you experience any kind of difficulty on account of anyone in the house then just let me know. My brother Duncan is rather smooth-tongued, and he's weak in some respects, but I know how to handle them. I won't have any nonsense.'

'I don't visualize any trouble,' Karen told him lightly.

'You don't know them,' he warned, watching her closely. 'I want you to know what you're up against. They'll fight you every minute, and you'll have to be on your guard all the time.'

'Perhaps you're exaggerating the situation,' she said.

'Think that if you wish.' He smiled slowly. 'Perhaps you do have enough charm to get by, but bear in mind what I've said, and remember that I'm somewhere around if you ever need anything. Duncan will probably tell you the same thing, but don't listen too closely to him.'

Karen nodded, but she was going to keep an open mind. She didn't know what the true situation in the house could be, and there might be deep animosity between these two sons. She wouldn't be surprised if one tried to play her against the other! It was something to guard against, and she returned to her unpacking while he talked, but now she didn't listen so closely to his words.

'I'm glad to see that my mother is in the hands of a qualified nurse,' he ended, getting to his feet when he became aware that he had lost her attention. 'I can trust you, Nurse Gregory. We're going to get along very well together.'

'I hope to achieve that with everyone in the house,' she retorted. 'Now if you'll excuse me I'll go to your mother. It must be almost time for her tea.'

'Don't be ruled by Amena,' he said, following her to the door. 'She'll try and overpower you, but remember what I said. No matter what you hear about me, I'm the best friend you'll have in this godforsaken house!'

Karen frowned at his words, and watched him as he went off along the corridor. He turned once to glance back at her, and when he smiled she felt warmed through to the heart. He was an intense man, and there didn't seem to be much wrong with him, despite what his brother Duncan had said about him. But Duncan himself had seemed strange, and she knew there could be some odd situation here involving the two brothers. But it was none of her business, she reflected. All she had to do was concern herself with Mrs Murray's health, and that was what she intended!

She went into the sick room and found Mrs Murray awake and staring at the window. The late summer afternoon was beginning to fade now, but there were several hours of sunlight left. For a moment Karen stared at the wan face on the pillows, and then Mrs Murray became aware of her and glanced in her direction. Karen glanced at her watch and went towards the bed. It was time she commenced her duties and set up some sort of routine! It was going to take her several days to discover all about her patient, but it was the kind of work for which she had trained, and she looked forward to the struggle of pulling this sick woman back into the ranks of the healthy . . .

'Nurse, I want to welcome you to my house,' Mrs Murray said slowly. 'Glen Hall hasn't been a very happy place, and I didn't want to get well again, but now that you're here I hope you'll be able to help me. Doctor Sloan says I can make it if I want to. Will you help me?'

'That's why I'm here, Mrs Murray. But don't tire yourself trying to talk now. We'll have a chat later. What would you like for your tea? I expect you've been getting your meals at a regular time, but now that I'm here I'll start a proper routine, and we'll stick to that no matter what.'

'I've lost all interest in food,' came the slow reply.

'Then let me see if I can tempt you.' Karen smiled warmly, and was gratified to see an answering smile appear on the woman's wan features. It wasn't going to be difficult at all, she told herself.

But when she went down to the kitchen she found a different atmosphere. Duncan Murray sat at the long wooden table, and Miss Ferguson was near him. Amena Lachlan was at the heavy stove, making tea. There was another man at the far end of the room, seated in a high-backed wooden chair placed to catch the light from the great high windows, and he was reading a newspaper. He was an oldish man, and after a glance at Karen, returned to his newsprint and did not pay her further attention.

'Do you want your tea?' the housekeeper demanded, and her tones suggested that Karen could take care of herself.

'Not yet, thank you,' Karen replied gently. 'I'm attending to Mrs Murray first.'

'I always take care of her food!' There was a challenge in the low pitched tones. 'You do the nursing and leave me to do my own duties.'

'My patient's food is my duty,' Karen said. 'I'll take care of it in my way.'

'We'll see about that! I've met your kind before!' The old housekeeper was angry. 'You haven't been in this house two hours and already you're trying to give me orders. Well it won't work here, I can tell you. Why they had to bother with a stranger in the house I'll never know. There are many in these parts who could do your job with no trouble at all, and without a lot of interference in what doesn't concern them.'

'Amena!' Duncan Murray's voice was harsh and determined. 'I have already told you that what Nurse Gregory does about my mother is her business. You do as she tells you in that respect. No-one is trying to undermine your authority in this house. Nurse Gregory hasn't the slightest interest in your affairs. You're always grumbling that you have far too much to do around here, so show that you're grateful at being relieved of caring for my mother. Do what you can to help the nurse! I'm sure we'll all feel happier if there is harmony in this kitchen.'

Karen glanced at him with appreciation showing in her blue eyes. What he had said was exactly what she wanted to convey to the housekeeper, but he merely smiled briefly and returned to his meal, and Karen glanced at the housekeeper, perturbed by the opposition showing in the woman's wrinkled face.

'If you're to take over the running of my kitchen then there's nothing I can do about it,' Mrs Lachlan said. 'But I protest. I object to this invasion.'

'Shut up, woman, do!' The old man by the window rustled his paper impatiently and glanced up at Karen. 'Her work has nothing to do with yours, no more than yours has to do with her. Let's have some peace in this house like the master says.'

'I might have known that you would go against your own wife,' Amena Lachlan said fiercely. 'You should remember that your loyalties lie with the poor sick woman in that room upstairs.'

'Spare us that, do,' Duncan Murray said angrily. 'I'm the master of this house and I've given instructions. They will be followed no matter what, and I'll be angry if Nurse Gregory reports obstruction on your part.'

'Very well! I didn't think I could rely on you for support. You've been hoping long enough that something would happen to drive me from this house. But don't forget your father's will, Duncan Murray.'

'That's something I shall never do,' he retorted, getting to his feet. He moved to the door with angry strides. 'Ever since he died you've been throwing it up in my face, and I'm getting heartily sick of your voice. If I have to take much more of it then you'll see just how difficult your own position here will become. It's about time someone gave you a little of your own medicine, Amena, and I'd like to see how well you can stand up to it.'

Duncan stalked out, and the housekeeper smiled thinly as she stared at Karen. Miss Ferguson tut-tutted and got to her feet, a small nervous woman with no desire to become embroiled in any unpleasantness. Karen watched her leave, and then she went to the stove, confronting the fierce old housekeeper and putting on a smile. She had to win over this woman or her life here would be one long ordeal!

'Mrs Lachlan,' she said in even tones. 'I'm here to do a job that you want to see come to a successful conclusion. The more help I get while I am here on the case the sooner Mrs Murray will be able to forget about this illness. That means I shall leave sooner, so why don't you help me to get done? I promise you I won't intrude upon your duties any more than I can help. I shall try to keep in the background, and I certainly have no desire to tread on your toes. I'm not interested in anything around here but the condition of my patient, and that's how it will be until the day I leave.'

'Trying to wheedle your way around me won't help,' the old woman said stubbornly. 'Do what you have to and I'll try not to interfere. But don't try to make a friend of me. You don't belong here. I could name a dozen women who have more right to be here. But nobody listens to me any more.' Her tones turned sorrowful. 'All right, so I don't care. Go right ahead with your duties. The mistress of the house is ill and needs help to regain her health. Although you're not my choice for the job it's obvious that you're going to stay. I'll not make your duties any more difficult.' There was a grudging acceptance beginning to sound now. 'Let me know what I can do to help.'

'Thank you.' Karen took care to keep triumph out of her tones. 'Mrs Murray's health is the only consideration, and I assure you that the quicker we put her back on her feet the better I shall like it.'

The old housekeeper nodded, and Karen prepared Mrs Murray's tea. She had won a victory, although it was uncertain, and she knew she had to hold on to the ground she had made. She could only show friendliness and hope that it would reap a harvest for her. It had worked before, but this particular situation had more than its share of tensions, and Karen could not help feeling that there was a lot more beneath the surface than showed. What the trouble was in this big old house she didn't want to know, unless it affected Mrs Murray's recovery. But she was going to take great care that the woman remained free of worry and had every opportunity to improve.

After taking care of her patient, Karen went back to the kitchen for her tea, and Amena Lachlan served her at the long wooden table. It seemed the whole family ate in the kitchen, and Karen wondered why so many of the large rooms in Glen Hall were not in use. But there was no-one to ask. Duncan and Roy Murray were not around, and the expression on the housekeeper's wrinkled face warned Karen that her hopes of a complete victory were still a long way from fruition. She would have to proceed carefully and hope for the best. It seemed that she would be here in Glen Hall for a matter of months, and during that time she had to make her life as comfortable as possible.

Later, she went back to the sick room, to find Mrs Murray asleep, and with nothing to do for a time, she decided to explore the extensive grounds around the house. She took a cardigan with her and left the house by the large front entrance. The evening sunshine was warm and gentle, but there were dark clouds upon the horizon, and a cool breeze blew in from the desolate moors beyond the high stone walls that surrounded the Hall. Karen walked along narrow paths that meandered through well kept lawns, and paused to admire the many flower beds. It was so peaceful that she could almost hear the clouds moving across the darkening sky, and when she paused by some bushes and turned to survey the great sprawling mass of the house she sensed that there was a strange brooding in the air. It was like the calm before the storm, and she shivered as some deep instinct moved within her.

For some moments she remained still, relaxing after the tensions of the day. She had travelled a great distance, and since her arrival there had been worries to contend with. Despite the housekeeper's apparent relenting of her harsh manner, Karen believed she wouldn't find much friendship and help, and she steeled herself to the knowledge that she would have to fend for herself while she was at Glen Hall.

A sudden rustling in the thick bushes at her back caused her to break her concentration, and she frowned as she turned and peered into the undergrowth that stretched back as far as the high wall. Some animal! The thought crossed her mind, and then she heard a low growl and she froze as an ominous shape loomed through the shadows. Her eyes widened when a large Alsatian confronted her, and the wild looking animal was growling far back in its throat. Its eyes seemed to glow redly, and there was such an intentness in their stare that Karen instintively realized that it was going to attack her.

But her good sense remained with

her despite the fear that tried to betray. She remained motionless, her hands behind her back, and she stared at the animal as it crouched before her like a tiger preparing to spring. She knew that if she made the slightest movement she would precipitate an attack, and the animal would be upon her before she could run to safety, even if there had been some refuge close at hand. She mentally consigned herself to the hands of God, and feared the worst . . .

3

How long Karen stood with the dog crouched at her feet she did not know, although it seemed a lifetime, but the animal remained staring at her with curiously bright eyes that seemed to warn that the slightest movement would bring attack. In reality only a few minutes passed before she heard a commanding whistle, and she took a deep breath and prepared to shout for help. But the slightest movement that she made brought a deep growl from the dog, and she refrained from calling. Presently she heard a noise somewhere in the bushes, and could not prevent herself turning her head in the hope of catching a glimpse of whoever was walking along the path there. The dog tremored, and seemed about to attack her. It growled loudly, and Karen subsided in fear, her heart pounding and her hands trembling behind her back.

'Blint, where the devil are you?' a voice called suddenly, very close at hand. 'Answer me, damn you!'

'Over here,' Karen said desperately in thin tones, and the dog growled menacingly and started to its feet, its whole body quivering with anticipation.

'Who's there?' Sudden alarm filled the man's voice, and Karen imagined it was Duncan Murray. Then she saw a slight movement in the bushes and felt relief seep into her breast as the tall figure of Roy Murray appeared. He looked at her in some surprise, then gazed at the dog, which did not relinquish its alert and frightening stare. 'Blint, you fool! What are you playing at? You're not a guard dog now! Get away and stop scaring Nurse Gregory!'

'Scaring me,' Karen said shakily. 'I was petrified! I thought he was going to attack me.'

'He might have done had you lost

your nerve and tried to run away,' Roy Murray said tightly. 'Why didn't you let me know you were going to make free use of the grounds? I would have introduced you to Blint and then it would have been all right. Come and say hallo to him now.'

Karen stared down at the dog, which sat now at Roy's side but was keeping her under steady surveillance, and she moved uncertainly towards him. The animal growled deep in its throat, and she paused and took a long, shuddering breath.

'Come on,' Roy said thinly. 'Show him fear and hesitation and he'll remember it.' He reached down and patted the dog. 'I want you to make friends with her, old boy,' he commanded. 'She's here to help the mistress. Shake hands with her, you old fool!'

The dog immediately held up a paw, and Karen stared in surprise. A moment ago it had been all set to tear her limb from limb. She looked down into its steady eyes, and went forward a pace to hold out her hand to the animal. The dog sniffed at her, then blinked, and she stretched out and patted it gently on the head, then rubbed a long ear.

'That's right,' Roy commented. 'Make friends with him. He does get out sometimes and roam the grounds, and it wouldn't be pleasant if he attacked you. But why didn't you mention that you wanted to come out for some air?'

'There was no-one I could tell,' Karen said firmly. 'I don't feel able to talk to the housekeeper. She hates the sight of me for some obscure reason.'

'She's like that with everyone, so don't feel honoured by her attitude.' He smiled thinly, and stood staring into her face with curious gaze.

Karen returned his stare, and there was the thought in her mind that his kiss had been pleasant and emotion-stirring. She tried to kill the thought, but the pleasure of that surprising moment lingered with her. She hadn't been kissed too often recently, and a thing like that made a great deal of speculation arise from it.

'Have you got a man somewhere?' he asked at length.

'A man?' She watched his face, considering that he was too handsome, and he probably knew it. He had more than likely given the local girls a run for their money! She smiled at the thought, and he pounced quickly.

'Are you smiling at me?' he demanded.

'No. It was something that came to mind, and had nothing to do with you.'

'Oh!' He seemed to relax. 'Come on, and I'll show you around the grounds. But remember to make friends with Blint and you'll be able to come and go as you please.'

'I certainly won't forget about him,' Karen said quickly, and bent to pat the dog's head. The animal licked her hand, and she sighed a little as she walked along at Roy's side. The dog stayed with her for a moment, then went off ahead, and they heard him rustling through the bushes. Karen suppressed a shudder. She wouldn't be able to forget that frightening incident when the dog had been prepared to attack her.

'Tell me something about yourself,' Roy commanded. 'Where do you come from? What's your life been like?'

'I come from London, or the suburbs, to be more precise,' she replied. 'I became a nurse as soon as I left school, and when I finished training I took up private nursing. My father is a dental surgeon in London.'

'And how old are you now?' He looked down into her eyes, and Karen smiled.

'A man shouldn't ask a girl her age,' she replied evasively.

'I don't believe in that rubbish. If I want to know about a girl then I want to know all about her.'

'I'm twenty-five, going on twenty-six!' Her blue eyes were bright as she smiled. 'Since this is the time for self-revelation, what about you?'

'I'm Roy Murray,' he said, grinning, and there was a glint in his dark brown eyes.

'Is that fact supposed to tell me all about you?' she questioned.

'If you were a local it would!'

'So you have a reputation!' She was speaking in a jocular tone. 'I should imagine that you have.'

'Impressions are never very accurate. You could be a long way from the truth!' He was still smiling, but there was a cold expression in his eyes. 'No doubt you'll hear quite a bit about me if you're here long enough, but don't pay too much attention to it because most of it won't be true.'

'And I should take your word for that?'

'Certainly.' He shook his head and bent to pick up a stick, calling to the dog, which appeared from the bushes so quickly that Karen could not prevent a start of surprise. 'Fetch it, Boy!' He flung the stick across the lawn and the dog went after it. 'I think I'd better warn you here and now that there is some family trouble going on. It doesn't affect you if you don't take sides.'

'I'm not likely to do that,' she retorted quickly. 'I'm here to nurse your mother, and that's all that concerns me. I can assure you that nothing will draw me into your troubles, whatever!'

'I'm glad to hear that! Perhaps we can be friends. I feel the need for a friend.'

'You're not married?' She glanced at his set face, then went on quickly. 'I shouldn't have asked that question. It's none of my business.'

'It is your business, and I've been asking you personal questions so why shouldn't you be curious?' He paused and stared after the dog. 'I am not married, and don't intend to be for a very long time. There are some who think I ought to have married years ago, but I'm only twenty-seven and I don't intend throwing away my freedom just yet.'

There was a trace of bitterness in his tones, and Karen could not help wondering at the trouble in his family, at which he had hinted. She'd got some impression from his brother that there was something of a cloud hanging over Roy Murray, although Duncan had not put it into so many words. She recalled the way the housekeeper had spoken to Duncan, and the old lady had mentioned that her position was secure at Glen Hall because of their father's will.

'Has Duncan spoken to you yet?' he demanded suddenly, and Karen jerked herself from her thoughts to reply.

'Only about my duties, and your mother's condition,' she said.

'He's always been close-mouthed. You won't get much out of him, but don't let him feed you any lies, Nurse Gregory.' He paused and looked down at her. She realized that her head came level with his shoulder.

'Why should he want to lie to me?'

'There is much you wouldn't understand. We're an old family and there are certain traditions that have not been observed. It was not my fault that tradition was broken, but I may very well take the blame. Duncan is unmarried, and ought to have been. As I am the younger son it doesn't matter so very much, and it's always been a rule that the eldest son of the family marries first.'

'Does that mean you would have married before now if you'd been able?' Karen watched his face closely, aware that tension was building up in him.

'No.' He smiled. 'But it saved me from making a fool of myself very badly some time ago!'

Karen smiled. He laughed, but there was no amusement in his voice. They walked on, and came to the large iron gates at the end of the drive. He glanced at his watch and then shut the gates, and Karen watched him, knowing that his mind was far from what he was doing. Blint came bounding up, and sat down at Karen's side, and she reached out and fondled the animal's head. He seemed to have forgotten completely that she had been a stranger some minutes ago, and the fact that Roy was friendly towards her made it all right for him to accept her.

'Do you always shut the gates at night?' she demanded.

'I do, when I'm here.' He came back to her side, and she watched his profile as he gazed around into the shadows.

'I suppose you work on the estate,' she continued.

'I am permitted to do some labouring now and again,' he retorted. 'But that doesn't suit Duncan. He'd be pleased if I went away and never came back.'

'Oh!' Karen could not prevent surprise from sounding in her voice, and he glanced down at her and smiled thinly.

'That surprises you! Well I said there were troubles in the family, didn't I? Come on, let's walk around the back of the house and lock Blint away for the night. I'd like to let him run loose through the grounds at night, but Duncan won't hear of it.'

'That could be dangerous,' Karen told him, recalling the fear she had felt at sight of the dog when it first appeared before her. 'Supposing some innocent person had to come to the house during the night.'

'Innocent person?' he queried.

'The doctor, for instance!'

'The dog knows him! Sloan would telephone, anyway, or someone would have called him.' He grinned. 'But you have more than your share of nerve, standing your ground when Blint came at you. A lot of people, especially girls, would have broken and run, much to their detriment. But how far does your nerve stretch? Are you afraid of old, gloomy houses?'

'Why? Is Glen Hall haunted?'

'You catch on quickly!' He nodded. 'I've seen something prowling the corridors. There's supposed to be the ghost of a long-dead piper around here. I've never heard him playing his weird music, as some people say, but I do believe we have something unnatural to boast of.'

'So long as he doesn't play the pipes then he won't worry me.' Karen smiled.

'You're not trying to frighten me now, are you?'

'No, just preparing you. It may not come as so much of a shock if you should see something unusual. You're going to do a great job here if you can nurse my mother back to full health. I'll do anything to help you.'

'Well you're not helping by trying to scare me.'

'You're not really afraid!' He smiled, looking frankly into her eyes. 'I shall be sleeping in the house while you're here, so don't worry, I'll always be at hand.'

'You haven't been sleeping at home then?'

'That's none of your business,' he rebuked sharply.

'Sorry. I thought we were being perfectly frank with one another this evening. You've asked me some very personal questions.'

'You've been at liberty to refuse to answer.' He was smiling again, and they walked along the drive and skirted the house. At the rear there were a number of outhouses, and some farm buildings down at the foot of a long slope. Karen caught a glimpse of a wide stretch of water lying between two towering mountains, and she caught her breath as the beauty of the scenery came to her.

'It's breath-taking the first time you set eyes upon it, isn't it?' he demanded, and there was pride in his tones. 'All this has been in my family for a great many years; more than three generations. But none of it is mine! My father didn't accept me as one of the family.'

'What?' Karen was shocked into asking the question, although it was more of an ejaculation. 'You're joking!'

'I wish that I were!' He shook his head. 'But forget about it. I shouldn't have mentioned it. I don't know what's getting into me now. Perhaps it's your pretty face loosening my tongue.'

'Perhaps I'd better go back to the house,' she said, and shivered. The breeze was turning spiteful now the sun was almost gone. 'I don't like to leave your mother very long at a time.'

'I can see that you're going to do your job thoroughly.' He nodded. 'I summed up your character that first moment I saw you.'

'I wouldn't have thought you had the time to do that — in the first minute.' She could feel colour coming into her cheeks at the memory. 'It was a most unusual greeting.'

'And fairly well out of character, for me,' he said briefly. 'I was acting as Duncan would have expected me to. But more of my reputation later.' He called to the dog and led it into a shed and bolted the door. 'I think you'll be perfectly safe with Blint in future, but it might be as well to let me know when you want to get some fresh air so I can accompany you. I'd hate for a nasty accident to happen.'

'I'll bear that in mind,' she said, nodding. They started back to the house, and he took her in through the kitchen door.

Amena Lachlan sat at the table,

sewing some dark material, and she looked up with some surprise as they appeared. The woman's dark eyes glinted momentarily, then quickly lost their interest and she returned her attention to the material. Roy did not speak, and led Karen through to the hall. There were dark shadows now, creeping into the corners, and an air of gloominess seemed to envelope Karen. She left Roy at the foot of the stairs and started up to Mrs Murray's room, pausing at the first landing to glance down to see where Roy was going. He went into the library, and she saw a light come on as she continued.

Mrs Murray was asleep, and Karen did not disturb the woman. She went into her own room and put the finishing touches to her unpacking. The room seemed hostile in some way, and she frowned as she switched on the light and then went to the windows to draw the heavy curtains. She had learned a lot from her conversation with Roy, but there was still a big mystery about the trouble within the family. She knew Roy's father's will figured prominently in the trouble, but there were other reasons for the apparent enmity between Roy and Duncan, and the two brothers and Amena Lachlan. But none of it would touch upon Karen's presence in the house, she was thankful to decide. Her task was relatively simple. She would take care of Mrs Murray, and leave when the woman no longer needed the services of a nurse.

Karen began to long for the time when she could go to bed. It had been a wearisome day, and now the pressures of arriving and trying to settle in had taken their toll of her nerves. But she had to settle Mrs Murray for the night, and later she took the woman some warm milk and gave her medicine. Soon after she went to her own room and prepared to go to bed. She left the communicating door open a little and retired, settling down in the big bed and almost instantly falling asleep. She knew nothing more until she awoke with a start early the next morning . . .

The following days were important ones for Karen, for she had to induce a routine which her patient would come to accept. But Mrs Murray proved to be a good patient, and there were no complaints from her about Karen's nursing. Life in the house seemed to settle to an uneasy serenity, and although the housekeeper kept her promise to do what she could to make Karen's job simpler, there was always that undercurrent of bad feeling which Karen could easily sense.

She saw little of either brother in the next few days, and for some reason that was a relief to Karen. She felt that she knew Roy a little better than Duncan because of their talk that first evening, but she tried to keep out of their way as much as possible. The doctor called regularly each day, and stayed to talk to Karen for as long as he was able, but he seemed to be a very busy man with a widely scattered practice, and he had to keep going in order to prevent his work piling up.

The only ray of light that came into the house was the maid, Deidre Stewart. Karen met her the very next morning when she went down to the kitchen to prepare Mrs Murray's breakfast. Amena Lachlan was there, of course, busy as usual, and the older woman seemed to resent the fact that there was someone of Karen's own age around to lighten the loneliness that closed in about her. Deidre was a local girl about twenty-four years of age, and she was a tall, slim brunette with wonderfully deep, dark eyes. Karen took to her at once, and when the girl greeted her there was warm friendliness in her gentle voice.

'But I'm very pleased to meet you, Nurse Gregory,' the girl said. 'I hope you'll like it here.'

Amena Lachlan sniffed loudly, and turned to the stove. Karen glanced at the old lady, but said nothing to her. She was going to show that she was not concerned by the atmosphere that surrounded them. But she felt that Deidre was going to be on her side, and she did what she could to make friends with the girl.

'I'm sure I'll like it here,' she replied slowly. 'I've never been in the Highlands before, but I have heard a lot about the hospitality of the Highlanders. I'm sure I'll settle down all right. But my welfare doesn't count, you know. When I'm on a case it's the patient, and only the patient, who counts.'

'That's dedication,' Deidre agreed with a smile. 'I don't think I would be good enough to become a nurse.'

'There are plenty in these parts who are good nurses, and every bit as capable as those modern people being trained in London,' the housekeeper said.

'You're thinking of your own,' Deidre said quickly, and pulled a face at the housekeeper's back. Karen could not suppress a smile, but she didn't want anyone taking sides in what might develop into a difficult situation. Harmony was the watchword, she knew, and she would have to do all the work to achieve it.'

'I'm sure Doctor Sloan did what he thought was best for Mrs Murray,' Karen said. 'As I said, she's the only one to be considered in this matter.'

'And I agree with you, Nurse.' The maid pulled out a chair. 'Are you coming to breakfast now?'

'No.' Karen smiled. 'I must attend to the patient first. Perhaps Mrs Lachlan will prepare the breakfast while I attend to Mrs Murray herself.'

'Aye! I'll do that, if you'll tell me what's to be done.' The housekeeper's tones were surly, but grudgingly respectful. Karen felt that they would make some improvement over the next few days, but if they didn't then there would be no hope at all for friendliness.

'Is there anything I can do to help?' Deidre demanded. 'I'd love to be in a position to do something.' She glanced towards the housekeeper. 'I'm never allowed in the sick room. I'll do the dusting in there if I may, Nurse.'

'I'll take care of the sick room,' Karen said. 'I'm sure you have more than enough to do in this large house, Deidre.'

'And she doesn't take the pains she's paid for,' Amena Lachlan said thinly.

Deidre caught Karen's eye and shrugged, and Karen smiled.

'You'd keep me busy all day, and all night, too, if I let you,' the girl retorted. 'You haven't done so much since I came here to work, Amena.'

'You call me Mrs Lachlan,' came the stern, unrelenting reply. 'When I was a girl in service there was a quality called respect. It's a pity there's none of it left in the world these days.'

Karen left the room, determined not to be drawn into anything that meant she might have to take sides. But she had the feeling that Deidre would help balance the situation in the house, and she was very pleased that the girl seemed so friendly. There was a lot she could learn from the maid, she thought, and looked forward to the time when she would be able to talk more freely to the girl. She needed to keep on top of her job, and vowed to use every effort to keep things just so. They wouldn't find her wanting in any respect, and she guessed that the housekeeper might well try to catch her out in some small neglect of duty. But she didn't intend for there to be any, and as she busied herself with the morning routine she held out high hopes for the future.

4

After several days, Duncan Murray sought out Karen to talk about her duties, and when he sent the maid for her Karen couldn't help wondering if something were wrong as she made her way to the spacious library. Tapping at the door, she heard his gruff invitation to enter, and opened the tall, heavy door and went into the room. She paused on the threshold and looked around admiringly, until Duncan called to her from his desk by one of the high windows, and then she closed the door and crossed to him.

'I wanted to talk to you about your hours, Nurse,' he said without preamble. 'I understand from Doctor Sloan that you work only a certain number of hours each week, and that you do have time off. No doubt you'll want a complete day off each week, in addition to a morning here and an afternoon there. Sit down please, and we'll discuss this matter. Perhaps I should have brought it up before. You've been with us almost a week already and you haven't had any time off.'

'I'm more concerned about your mother than my time off,' Karen replied immediately. 'I'll take my time off later, when she has shown some improvement.'

'The Doctor tells me she is already showing great improvement, and that it is thanks to you for the way you're attending her. I want to thank you, Nurse, for doing such a good job.'

'Your mother's progress is thanks enough for me,' Karen told him lightly. 'I'm so glad I get along so well with her.'

'Yes. You certainly do that. It's surprising how my mother has taken to you. I didn't think it would work, although I agreed with Doctor Sloan's suggestion that a trainee nurse would work wonders here. I hope you're getting along as well with the rest of the staff here. Mrs Lachlan isn't making your life a misery, is she?'

'No.' Karen shook her head and smiled. 'I thought she was going to be difficult, but she mellowed when she saw that I was interested only in getting your mother through this bad patch. I don't have any trouble at all.'

'And what about my brother?' He paused and regarded her in silence for a moment. 'Has he made any advances towards you, Nurse?'

'Advances?' Karen repeated. 'What do you mean?'

'No doubt Deidre has told you all about the various members of this household,' he went on diffidently. 'We are a strange assortment, if everything is to be believed. But Roy is the worst of us all, and he won't respect your position here if he decides to have some fun at your expense.'

'I haven't seen your brother since I arrived,' Karen said firmly. 'On the occasion when I did meet him in the grounds he treated me with the greatest respect.'

'Of course there are days when he is on his best behaviour!' Duncan smiled thinly.

'And the maid hasn't confided in me about the lives of anyone in the house!' There was a thin smile of warning on Karen's face, and he nodded slowly.

'I didn't intend to convey that I suspect her of standing around all day just gossiping,' he said. 'But no doubt there is a lot about this place that you ought to know, and the maid is the most suitable person to tell you. Now let's get back to the point. Would you like a regular day off each week, or take a day each week when it suits you?' He paused and took a deep breath. 'I must tell you that there's quite a lot for you to see in this area. The town of Glen Tay is only ten miles from here, and of course you saw the village of Loch Tor when you arrived. There's not so much in the village to interest a girl like you, but any time you want to go into town you have only to say so and I'll arrange transport for you. I'm afraid the bus service in these parts is very erratic, and certainly not scheduled for the convenience of the passengers.'

'Thank you. I think it would be better if I took a day when I thought it convenient,' Karen said. 'Who will attend your mother when I am off duty?'

'The housekeeper and the maid will do what they did before you arrived. They'll be able to cope for one day each week.'

'Very well. I'll let you know the evening before, shall I, when I want to take some time off?'

'If you would I shall be able to make the necessary arrangements in time,' he replied. 'Thank you for being so easy to please.'

'It's my place to see that everything goes off simply,' Karen told him. 'It saves a lot of trouble all round in the long run.'

'I wish some of the others in this house had the same attitude, Nurse,' he said, smiling thinly. He got to his feet, intimating that the meeting was over, and as she arose he escorted her to the door.

Karen thought about him as she went back to the sick room. There was a defensive air about him, as if he were permanently on guard against showing emotion of any kind. She found herself beginning to wonder about the true situation, and had to make an effort not to start guessing at the undercurrents so obviously flowing through the affairs of the house and all who lived in it.

Mrs Murray seemed a lot better today, she thought, after giving the woman her mid-morning dose of medicine. In the four days that she had been at Glen Hall, the woman had come from silent approval to muttered phrases intended to show agreement and acceptance. But this morning, after lying back thankfully, pulling a wry face at the taste of the medicine, Mrs

Murray held Karen's attention with her deep gaze.

'Is there anything else I can do for you, Mrs Murray?' Karen demanded. 'You're quite comfortable, aren't you? Would you like an extra pillow now, so you can sit up a little and look out the window?'

'No thank you! Perhaps later. I would like to talk to you, though. I'm sorry that I had adverse thoughts about you when you first arrived, and I didn't want you here in the first place. But now that you've been here these few days I want to tell you how glad I am that you came.'

'Thank you, Mrs Murray.' Karen smiled happily and brought forward a chair to sit down beside the bed where the woman could see her easily. 'I'm sure you'll make a lot of progress now. Doctor Sloan is pleased with the way you're showing more interest already.'

'There was a time when I wished I would die!' The words were little more than a whisper, and a shadow crossed the woman's wan face.

'Everyone feels like that after a serious illness,' Karen said encouragingly. 'But you're looking forward now to the time you'll be able to get up, aren't you?'

'I think I am!' Mrs Murray's dark eyes held Karen's gaze. 'I'm sure I'll be able to face the future with more confidence by the time I am able to stir. Have you met both my sons now?'

'Yes. I was talking to Duncan a short time ago, and I have met Roy, although he hasn't been around since the day I arrived.' A frown touched Karen's face, for she remembered Roy's words that he would be around now that she was here. But perhaps he was in the house even though she hadn't seen him.

'Duncan is a very dependable man! Roy has caused me a lot of trouble! But it is Roy I am most concerned about!'

'That's usually the case.' Karen smiled gently. 'A mother worries more about the son who gives her a good reason.'

'He's never been a bad one!' Mrs Murray spoke fiercely, and pride shone momentarily in her brown eyes. 'There are some who would say I'm blind where Roy is concerned, but I know my sons, and there is no badness in Roy. Perhaps he's been a little wild, but his father was to blame for that. What happened in the past should be overlooked, shouldn't it?'

'I'm sure we all have episodes in our past which are better overlooked,' Karen said diplomatically.

'It's a tonic just to talk to you!' Mrs Murray nodded her approval. 'But one of my reasons for not wanting a nurse in the house was what happened when my husband's nurse was here. He lay ill for six months before he died, and a local girl nursed him. Both Duncan and Roy were in love with her, and after my husband's death there was a great deal of trouble before she went away and never returned.'

Karen tensed as she listened. So that was the root cause of some of the unpleasantness she had encountered upon arrival. And perhaps that was why Roy had kissed her that moment he met her. Perhaps he had been trying to make headway on his brother! She took a swift breath at that thought, then mentally decided that neither brother would have any interest in her. Roy had stayed out of her sight since that first day, and her encounter with Duncan a short time ago had hardly been inspiring. But what Mrs Murray had told her certainly accounted for the bad blood which seemed to exist between the brothers. Nothing could stir up trouble between two men like a woman, the same woman in both their minds. It might even explain Amena Lachlan's attitude towards her.

'You're not married, are you, Nurse?'

'No, Mrs Murray.'

'And is there a man in your life?'

'Not at the moment.' Karen smiled gently. She knew what it was like to lose a loved one. She could understand the deep emotions that must have been aroused between Duncan and Roy Murray. Love was the most powerful of all emotions. It absorbed every living fibre and involved itself in each thought and action.

'You're not finding it lonely here, are you?' There was an urgency showing in the woman's pale cheeks.

'My work is sufficient to me,' Karen replied. 'I'm quite happy here, and anything beyond nursing you doesn't count with me.'

'But you are a young woman, and you need to get out and about as often as possible. I shall order Duncan to take you into town when he can.'

'We've already talked about my days off duty,' Karen told her. 'It's all arranged.'

'There's no need for you to wait until your day off. I don't need nursing in the evenings. You must have some relaxation. I'm sure the heavy atmosphere of this old house weighs heavily upon you. I can remember when I first came here. I was little more than a girl then, and it took me years to get accustomed to this place and all its customs.' The voice grew fainter. 'It's all so very long ago now. Time has stolen away and left me nothing but my memories.'

'Try to rest now, Mrs Murray, and we'll talk again later. I'm sure you have some very interesting tales to tell about Glen Hall, and I shall be delighted to hear them. But you mustn't tire yourself out. Rest now and you'll feel even brighter tomorrow. I can see the improvement you're making. In a short time you will be getting up for a period each day.'

'Thank you, Nurse. It's a comfort having you here. I must thank Doctor Sloan when he arrives today. He talked me into having a nurse here, and I needed some persuasion, I can tell you.'

'Well I'll leave you to sleep until it's time for lunch,' Karen said. 'Try to sleep a little. Each day will see you getting a bit better, and we'll soon have you back on your feet.'

'I do feel a lot better already,' the

woman admitted. She sighed and closed her eyes, and Karen watched her face for a moment before turning and leaving the room.

There was relief in Karen as she went into her own room, to find Deidre there cleaning. Everything seemed to be working out. Now Mrs Murray was beginning to talk about herself there was every chance that the woman would completely recover from her illness. There were phases to recovery, and now Karen knew them all. She was quick to recognise this first phase, and was ready to do all she could to encourage it.

'Anything wrong, Nurse?' the maid demanded 'You're looking very thoughtful.'

'Wrong?' Karen shook her head. 'No, Deidre, I was just thinking about Mrs Murray's condition. She's beginning to show a lot of improvement.'

'Good. I'm glad to hear that!' The girl's brown eyes were warm and friendly. 'She's such a wonderful woman. There were times when I thought she was going to die. It would have been a great tragedy. She deserves some happiness before her end. She's had a hard life.'

'With her husband, do you mean?' Karen wasn't just curious. She wanted to know about Mrs Murray's past because it might help her nurse the woman. A deeper understanding of the patient's life was never a waste of effort.

'He was a dreadful man!' Deidre Stewart shook her head and sat down on the foot of Karen's bed. 'What Mrs Murray ever saw in him I'll never know. I was afraid of him. He had such intense brown eyes, and you wouldn't think it possible that a human could put so much expression into his eyes. Roy takes after him to some extent, although Roy isn't harsh or bad.'

'Are you saying that his father was bad?'

'Bad in a moral sense. He didn't care for people's feelings. His own family were just puppets, to be used as and when he wanted. He didn't allow for emotion, and Roy and Duncan had no say in anything. They had to do as they were told.'

'I can imagine Duncan knuckling under,' Karen said, 'but not Roy!'

'And you're quite right.' The maid smiled as she nodded. 'You can judge character, Nurse. Duncan did as he was told, but Roy gave his mother a lot of grief because he stood up to his father, and that took a lot of nerve, I can tell you. Why, Roy even lifted his hands to his father once, when he thought the old man was going to hit his mother. I believe the old man respected him for his spirit, but he punished him severely.'

'That's why they say Roy was troublesome, is it?' Karen was getting a clearer picture of the man now. 'I thought he'd made trouble in the usual ways open to a rich man's son.'

'Roy didn't get into trouble of his own free will!' Deidre's eyes gleamed with suppressed passion. 'He's too sensitive to other people's feelings. But I wouldn't trust Duncan even if I had to. There's something hard and cold about him. I think he was so afraid of his father that he let his emotions die. Now he can't help himself. I was surprised when he fell in love with his father's nurse.'

'Mrs Murray was saying something about that.' Karen hoped she would now hear the full story, but Deidre got to her feet and moved to the door.

'I wouldn't want to talk about it in this house,' she said. 'It would be more than my job is worth to let Duncan or Roy hear me talking about it.'

'Was it as bad as that?' Karen was disappointed, although she kept her tones casual.

'It was just short of murder, I do believe!' The girl's eyes glinted for a moment. 'It was a dreadful time for everyone. What with the master's death, and the will, when it became known! No wonder Mrs Murray nearly died!'

Karen was disappointed as the maid departed, for her curiosity was aroused. But now she knew the extent of the trouble that existed in the family, and she did not wonder that Mrs Murray was ill, as the maid had said. She thought of the housekeeper, and could not help considering that Amena Lachlan had some kind of a hold on the household because of the will that had been left. But what kind of a man had the father really been?

She went down to the kitchen to get her morning coffee, and Amena Lachlan eyed her furtively, breaking off a conversation with Roy Murray.

'Coffee, Nurse?' Roy enquired.

'Yes please,' Karen nodded and smiled.

'I'll get it,' the housekeeper said thinly.

'How is my mother this morning?' Roy continued, coming to her side, and Karen found herself wondering what kind of a man he really was deep down inside as she replied lightly.

'She's much better this morning. I think we'll have her up on her feet in a very short time.'

'I wouldn't be too optimistic,' Amena Lachlan said from the front of the stove. 'Sick people have their ups and downs, you know.'

'I'm sure Nurse Gregory knows what she is talking about,' Roy said tersely. His jaw jutted a little, Karen noticed. 'Why do you have to be so nasty to everyone, Amena? In all the years I've known you, I don't believe you've ever said a kind word for anyone outside of your own family.'

'I'll have none of that in my own kitchen,' the old lady said irritably. 'If you want, I'll bring your coffee into the library.' She smiled thinly, and Karen saw a malicious expression cross her face.

'You know I never use the library,' Roy said angrily. 'It's where Duncan works. But you can bring it into the front lounge. Come along, Nurse. I do want to talk to you, and this will be an admirable moment.'

Karen felt that she ought to protest, but she did not, and permitted herself to be led from the kitchen. The sun was shining through the high windows of the large room in the front of the house, and Roy led her across to one of the windows and they stood gazing out across the wide extent of smooth lawns.

'That old woman!' he said with great feeling. 'Why the devil my father took such a fancy to her I'll never know.' He smiled bitterly. 'Unless he figured that she would continue where he left off.' He looked down at her, and Karen saw emotion in his eyes, but the light died as she watched, and he set his teeth and shook his head. 'Has Duncan spoken to you about your time off duty?' he demanded.

'Yes.' She inclined her head, then explained what had been arranged.

'I'll drive you into town any time you want to go,' he said. 'I don't do anything around the estate. Duncan is capable all by himself! I suppose he has said that he'll drive you in?'

'He said he would arrange it!' Karen could sense the bitterness that lay deep in him, and wondered what had happened between these brothers. Who had been to blame for the trouble which erupted over the previous nurse? Had both men been in love with her? And what kind of a nurse had she been to let her personal life intrude into her nursing?

'I'd like to take you out one evening when you're free,' he went on steadily. 'You need someone who knows the countryside to show you around. The moors are particularly beautiful at this time, and if you've never seen them before then you've got a treat awaiting you.' He paused again, and glanced at her, and Karen kept her gaze on the scene beyond the window, conscious of his attentive gaze but not wanting to meet it. 'Has Duncan said he would take you out?'

'No.' Karen spoke more harshly than she intended. She sighed slightly as she turned to face him. But before she could speak there was a tap at the door and the housekeeper entered, carrying a tray.

'Put it down on the table, Amena,'

Roy said impatiently, and the old lady sniffed loudly as she did so. She slammed the door as she departed.

'She's a pleasant old soul!' Roy remarked, and laughed harshly. 'Come and drink your coffee before it turns cold, and let's hope that Amena hasn't poisoned it.'

'That's a shocking thing to say!' Karen looked up into his eyes and saw something of the real man in their dark depths. She felt an indefinable stirring deep within her breast, and was forced to breathe deeply to rid herself of some of the tension that quickly built up.

'You must have learned by now that I'm a shocking man!'

'You seem concerned that people will talk about you behind your back,' she countered, taking up a cup of coffee from the tray and moving to a seat. He joined her without answering, and she was too aware of his nearness, but did not move.

'I don't care what people say about me,' he replied carelessly. 'I've become accustomed to all that. It doesn't hurt me, and most of it isn't the truth. But what about you? What makes you tick? I'm interested to know.'

'Why?' Karen threw the word at him.

'Why not? You're a beautiful girl who has come to live among us! I'd be a poor specimen of man if I didn't show interest.'

'I'm a dedicated nurse,' she replied softly. 'I don't mix my profession with my personal life. The two are kept very far apart. That's the only reason why I won't go out with you or your brother.'

'So someone has been telling you about the past.' His voice had thickened, and was barely recognizable. 'What happened before has nothing to do with the present situation.'

'I don't know what happened before.'

'Then I'll tell you.' He faced her, suddenly determined, and there was great strength of character in his expression.

'I would rather not hear, thank you. I don't want to become involved. I have a very important job in this house, and I won't permit anything to come between me and my duty.'

He was silent for a moment, and his passions were slowly subsiding. Then he nodded, and the rest of the tension went out of him. 'I admire you,' he said slowly. 'I don't think I've ever met a girl like you before.'

'I expect you say that to all the girls,' she retorted lightly, trying to relieve the atmosphere which had settled over the room. She was glad to see a smile come to his lips. He nodded slowly, then sat back and drank his coffee.

'I can wait,' he told her presently. 'You're new here yet. I can wait until you settle in. Then I'm going to show you what I'm really like. I have a feeling about you, Nurse Gregory, and no matter what your attitude is at the moment, you're going to change it drastically in future.' He paused and thinned his lips for a moment, looking very handsome and attractive in a dark, over-powering way. 'This time it will be different,' he promised. 'I won't let anything stand in my path. I've fallen in love with you and I'm certain you could feel something for me. But I'm willing to be patient. You'll see!'

5

Karen was so astonished by his words that she almost choked on her coffee. But before she could recover from her surprise he had got to his feet and left the room, leaving her sitting and staring at the door after him. She arose from her seat and set down her cup, then walked to the window to stand and ponder over his words. She had been in the house four days! In that time she had been too busy to consider what effect his kiss had made upon her, but now his words had released some sort of a lock in her brain and all her pent up emotions came pouring out into prominence. She could actually feel a tingle in her lips, as if he had kissed her again!

But she was being absurd! She tried to break the hold his words had placed upon her. Being alone, strange and uncertain in such a large house, had filled her with a sense of loneliness that had never gripped her before. She was actually yearning for some kind of human contact, something which would prove stronger than the nurse-patient relationship she had with Mrs Murray. But she was not the type to want romance or love, or anything even remotely connected with them. She had learned her lesson a long time ago.

Karen remained lost in thought until the door opened and disturbed her, and she saw Amena Lachlan entering. The housekeeper paused to look around, and her seamed face showed surprise that Karen was alone. But she collected the tray and departed without comment, and Karen followed her from the room and went up to check Mrs Murray.

There was nothing for her to do until lunch, and she glanced at her watch and found she had an hour to spare. A breath of fresh air would blow away the cobwebs in her mind, she decided, and fetched her cardigan after looking in on her patient and finding her asleep. She went out to the gardens, and breathed deeply of the keen air as she walked slowly in the sunlight. There was much on her mind to be sorted out. But she didn't know where to start with her spring-cleaning. Roy Murray's words had done something to those mysterious processes which worked automatically inside her head.

She sighed as she suddenly visualized complications coming into her well ordered life. She had always made it a golden rule that she did not become personally involved either with her patients or any member of their families. A girl who could not keep herself in the background would not last long as a private nurse. But Roy Murray had somehow slipped through her guard, and she realized that the kiss with which he had greeted her on the day of her arrival had affected some change on her that no other man had managed to do.

'Excuse me!' The harsh voice spoke

from the bushes, and Karen almost jumped out of her skin in surprise. She turned, to see Robert Lachlan standing in the shadows, holding pruning shears in one thickly gloved hand.

'Good morning,' Karen said instinctively. 'It's a nice day for your work.'

'Aye.' He nodded, a tall thin man with shrewd blue eyes that took in every detail of Karen's lithe figure. He had a gentleness in his face that could have been born of resignation, and thinking of his wife Amena, Karen could feel only pity for him. But he hadn't spoken to her before in the four days she had been here, and they had passed each other often in the big house. She saw him glance towards the house as if afraid that his wife might be watching, and Karen could not resist a glance in the same direction. 'How is Mrs Murray these days?' he demanded furtively.

'She's much better!' Karen relaxed a little. 'I think we shall soon be seeing her out of bed and moving around the house. If she continues to make progress then my stay here will be very short indeed!'

'I just want to say I'm glad they sent you here. That Doctor Sloan has got a lot of sense. If my wife had had her way — !' He broke off and half turned back to his work, and Karen watched his hands as he pruned some of the many rose bushes. She became absorbed in what he was doing, and didn't notice that he glanced at her from time to time.

'Do you take care of all the gardens here?' she demanded at length.

'Aye!' There was pride in his tones. 'When the old master was alive I served as the butler in the house, but since he passed on I've got out here where I can do much good.' He paused in his work to study her face for a moment. 'Do you like it here?'

'I haven't had a chance to look at the countryside, but I'm sure I shall love it when the opportunity arrives for me to get out. At the moment I'm only concerned with Mrs Murray's condition, and I'm very pleased about her.'

'Aye, she's a grand woman! It would be a great pity if she didn't pull through this bad patch. I wish you success, Nurse Gregory.'

His speech held a thick accent at times, making it difficult for Karen to understand fully what he said, but she nodded, getting his general meaning plainly enough. She smiled lightly as she replied.

'I haven't lost a patient yet, Mr Lachlan. I sincerely hope that I won't spoil my record with Mrs Murray.'

'She's a strong woman for all her appearances,' he retorted. 'She had to be to put up with her life's worries. What do you make of the two men of the house, eh? They're not after bothering you at all, surely!'

'I see very little of either of them.' Karen made to move on, not wanting to follow the natural course the conversation was taking. But she was aware of a strange desire to know more about Roy

Murray welling up inside her and she tried to fight it off. She couldn't ask questions! That would betray her interest. She would learn all she needed to know in time, and she would have to control her impatience. 'Isn't that the doctor's car?' she demanded in some relief as she glanced towards the drive at the sound of a vehicle.

'That's him!' Lachlan pulled a face, obviously disappointed that their conversation could not go on. 'I hope to see more of you out here, Nurse. Perhaps we might find some interesting things to talk about.'

'I love gardening, Mr Lachlan,' she responded. 'I shall certainly try to get out here as often as possible.'

She started away from him, and watched the large black car moving up to the house. It stopped short of the sprawling building, and then Doctor Sloan got out. He had spotted her, and was waiting for her to join him. She hurried, and was breathless when she reached his side.

'Taking the air?' he demanded jovially. 'I'm glad to see you getting some excercise. There's colour in your cheeks this morning, and yesterday you seemed pale and overwrought. You're not getting any trouble in the house, are you?'

'None at all, and Mrs Murray certainly looks a lot better today,' she replied. 'We're making good progress, Doctor.'

'I had the feeling that a nurse in here would do the trick,' he said, nodding. She watched him glance at his watch. 'I've got a little time to spare, Nurse, so let's stroll through the gardens and talk about this case. I'm sure there are some things you should be aware of which haven't been brought to your notice. I am responsible for you being here, and I take my responsibilities very seriously.'

'I must confess there are some things here which puzzle me, but they don't have any direct bearing upon the case itself,' she said as they walked along a path that skirted the house.

'You can never tell!' He glanced at

her, smiling thinly, a tall, handsome man with very blue eyes and long, fair hair that curled around his ears and the nape of his neck. He couldn't be more than thirty, she believed, but there was a worldliness about him that made him seem much older.

'Well I like to learn as much as possible about the patient's life,' Karen said. 'I don't think a nurse's job is just to make the patient comfortable and to administer the medicine. If there are provoking circumstances in the patient's life that either helped the illness or retards recovery, then I think the nurse must do all she can to remove the causes.'

'You're the type of nurse I'm always pleased to work with,' he said with a satisfied smile. 'Needless to say, I agree completely with your attitude towards nursing. And in this particular case you will find enough to try and put right for the patient's sake. I don't know if I have enough time in which to tell you fully all the wrong things that have contributed to Mrs Murray's illness. She's had a hard life, and conditions were aggravated by her husband's complete lack of sensitivity and emotion. I never met a harsher man, Nurse, and he had this entire household completely under his thumb. It was the release caused by his death that threw Mrs Murray into her illness, but even after his death the master left trouble for her. His will was a masterpiece of contrived spitefulness that has harmed each one of the family and the staff.'

'I have heard some mention of it, but not exactly what happened,' Karen admitted.

'There's no understanding a man with the mind Hector Murray had,' Doctor Sloan went on. 'He provided for his family in the will he left, but he also provided for the Lachlans, and he gave them a share of the estate. Duncan Murray contested the will, but was overruled, and that's why there's so much bitterness in the house at the moment. Mrs Murray was torn between two loyalties. She knew she had to do the right thing by her sons, and at the same time she wanted to honour her dead husband's last wishes. I think it was that situation which brought about her illness more than any other aspect of the whole business. The years of torment she lived here didn't seem to contribute to her condition, but the fact that Hector Murray left a legacy of distrust and hatred in Glen Hall after his death seemed to be the final straw.'

'I can well imagine!' Karen shook her head slowly, considering what she had learned. 'It must have been very troubling for her to know that Amena Lachlan was a part owner of the Hall.'

'Among other things!' Sloan eyed her lovely face speculatively. 'Amena is secure in her job at the Hall for as long as she lives, and she cannot help reminding the brothers of the fact. I've heard her myself. But that isn't the end of it. I believe Hector Murray had the mind of the Devil himself. He knew the situation wouldn't stop growing, and just lately I've begun to fear that the worst might happen. There was a lot of trouble here after Hector Murray died. His nurse was a young woman and she fell in love with Roy. He didn't seem to care much about her, but she was persistent, and as soon as he began to show interest in her she turned to Duncan. There was a terrific row here, and that was the night Mrs Murray collapsed.'

'It must have been dreadful for her,' Karen said slowly.

'I was a regular visitor to the Hall by then,' he went on. 'I knew all of them pretty closely, and I thought there would have been murder done, but the nurse went her way and the two men have settled down again, but there's no love lost between them now. Roy has always been a bit wild — nothing bad about him, you understand, but he's inclined to go his own way no matter the consequences, and he came off worse in this will that was left. He has no say in the estate, and since his father's death he's lost what little interest he did have in the place. But he loves his mother, and I believe she is the only reason why he still sticks around here.'

'I see.' Karen was thoughtful. The doctor's words were like drops of molten lead in her mind. Now she could begin to grasp the picture of what life was like in Glen Hall. She couldn't help wondering what kind of a man Hector Murray had been, and it was clear to her that Roy and Duncan were living under an intolerable strain. Their father must have been a most unloving and ungenerous man, and she could not help wondering if the same characteristics would show in either son.

'I've painted a gloomy picture,' Doctor Sloan said, 'but I felt that you should be in possession of the more pertinent facts. I would be doing less than my duty if I didn't prepare you for the situation. None of this should affect you, I agree, but it is better to be informed, don't you think?'

'Yes, Doctor, and thank you. I shall remember what you've told me.'

'So now we can be on our way to a more cheerful subject!' He was smiling, and the sunlight was glittering in his pale blue eyes. 'Have you arranged your off duty periods yet? You haven't, to my certain knowledge, been out of the house since you arrived, and this is the fifth day. I suggest you arrange to take this evening off and I'll call for you at about seven and take you out. Does that appeal to you?'

'Why, I — !' Karen paused, more than a little surprised by his unexpected offer, and he heaved a sigh and shook his head.

'Most people seem to look upon a doctor as being a little less than human,' he observed. 'But I am a bachelor, only twenty-nine years of age, and there's no girl in my life. I'm in partnership with a very old local doctor who was once a friend of my father's. He doesn't leave the house very often, apart from duty, and he expects me to be the same. I'd very much appreciate it if you gave me a reason for getting out.'

'Very well then, I'd be delighted to go out with you,' Karen said lightly. 'I'd better have a word with Duncan before you leave, just in case it isn't suitable this evening.'

'Well I have this afternoon and evening free,' he said. 'I had better see Mrs Murray now, then get on with the rest of my round. But you talk to Duncan immediately, and then I'll know what we can plan.'

They turned and retraced their steps to the house, and Karen was filled with conjecture. She felt uplifted by the thought of getting away from Glen Hall for a time, if only for a matter of hours. The house had an overpowering atmosphere about it, and she wondered if the accumulated hatreds of Hector Murray's lifetime continued to live on in the rooms of the old building. Doctor Sloan opened the door and stepped aside for her to enter. Then he crossed the threshold and started up the stairs while Karen went along to the library and tapped gently at the door.

'Come in!' Duncan Murray's tones were cold and distant, and Karen entered the large room and walked slowly towards the desk where he sat. He was busy on the estate accounts, and for a moment she stood looking down at him, taking in his solid profile, while he calculated a list of figures. He made some entries at the bottom of the column, then turned to look up at her. 'Anything wrong, Nurse?' he demanded unemotionally, and she had the feeling that if she said the house was on fire he would refer her to the housekeeper, or his brother.

'We were talking about my off-duty periods earlier,' she said. 'Would it be all right if I had this evening off?'

'This evening?' He pulled a face. 'You've been talking to Roy. Has he asked you out?'

'No.' She shook her head.

'Oh!' He seemed relieved. 'Then of course it will be all right.'

She had the feeling that he would have refused her had she said she was going out with his brother. But she did not let her face change expression as she spoke. 'Thank you. Would it be convenient if I left here at about seven?'

'That will be all right. What about transport? We're in a remote spot here.'

'That's being taken care of! I shall be picked up here and returned later.'

'Good. It wouldn't do to attempt walking anywhere. A city girl wouldn't get very far.'

'I agree with you.' Karen could see he was anxious to get back to his work. 'I'm sorry if I interrupted your calculations,' she added as she moved towards the door.

'Think nothing of it.' He smiled, and his face seemed to come alive. 'I sometimes think I work too hard at this business. Perhaps we can arrange to have an evening out together shortly.'

Karen did not answer. She was almost at the door, and she could imagine how their trouble started with the previous nurse. But she could not encourage either brother, and give them no ground for dissention. She paused in the doorway and glanced back at him, and Duncan was watching her with something like yearning on his fleshy face.

'Thank you, Mr Murray,' she said sweetly, and departed, closing the door gently. She paused in the hall and took a deep breath, then sighed heavily. Her steps were heavy as she ascended the stairs to the sick room, but she had the first slim hopes of friendship with Doctor Sloan. That would successfully hold the Murray brothers at bay, and the doctor was a handsome, attractive and well mannered man who would make a suitable companion during her stay here. She decided to cultivate a friendship with the doctor, and with that intent firmly fixed in her mind she entered Mrs Murray's room to find him talking to the patient.

Later, when they walked down to the hall together, Karen told Phelan Sloan that she would be able to meet him that evening, and his smile of appreciation filled her with pleasure. They made final arrangements and then he departed, and as she watched him go, Karen was filled with strange anticipation. She felt very light hearted and high spirited, and the time couldn't pass quickly enough for her. With lunch behind her, she was faced with a long afternoon, and the hours seemed to conspire against her and time seemed to halt. But with its usual inexorable movement, the afternoon did fade away, and Karen was greatly relieved when she had tea behind her and could think about preparing for the evening.

When Deidre came to tell Karen that Doctor Sloan had arrived the girl seemed to be bursting with curiosity and excitement. She paused in the doorway and eyed Karen, who was dressed in a pale blue dress and short coat.

'You look fit to kill!' the girl said enviously. 'And I like the way you do your hair. I wish I were blonde! But I wouldn't dye my hair for anything.'

'You've got such beautiful hair!' Karen said immediately. 'Anything you did to it would only spoil it, Deidre.'

'It's kind of you to say so!' The girl's brown eyes sparkled. 'But don't keep the doctor waiting. Go and enjoy yourself. You deserve it after being cooped up in this place for almost a week. I shall be taking care of Mrs Murray this evening, so don't worry about a thing. I'll be nearby all the time.'

'You must give her a dose of this medicine at about nine,' Karen said, crossing to a cabinet and opening the small door to reveal all the medicines kept there. She moved the bottle in question to the front of the cabinet. 'Give her a sleeping tablet at nine-thirty.'

'I know all about her medicines,' the girl said. 'I used to look after her occasionally before you came.'

'Then she'll be in good hands!' Karen relaxed a little. 'I was worried about going out and leaving her.'

'Have a nice time, and forget about this place until it is time for you to come back! May I watch you go from the window?'

'Of course!' Karen smiled and took up her handbag and gloves and hurried from the room. She entered the sick room and approached the bed. Mrs Murray was awake, and the woman smiled when she saw Karen at her best. 'I'm leaving now, Mrs Murray,' Karen told her. 'Is there anything you want before I go?'

'Nothing at all. Deidre can attend me until you come back. Have a nice time and forget about Glen Hall until you have to come back.'

'I shall hardly be able to do that,' Karen said gently. 'But I shall enjoy the evening.'

The older woman smiled, and Karen departed, hurrying down the stairs to where Doctor Sloan was waiting in the hall. He looked up at her as she descended, and when she neared him she could see the admiration and approval in his pale eyes. He came forward to be at the bottom stair as she reached him, and for a moment she paused and stared into his eyes.

'You're a picture!' he said slowly. 'This gloomy old house can't do you justice, but it does make you look like a gem in an old fashioned setting.'

'Thank you.' Pleasure welled up in Karen's heart, and she joined him and they crossed to the door. As the doctor opened it a harsh voice called from beyond the stairs, and Karen turned to see Amena Lachlan standing there.

'Have you no instructions for me to take care of the mistress?' the woman demanded.

'I understand that Deidre will be standing by until I return,' Karen said. 'I've given her full instructions.'

'She's only the maid here,' came the spiteful retort. 'I'm in charge of the house, and I give the orders.'

'But not where Mrs Murray is concerned,' Doctor Sloan said loudly.

'She doesn't come under your ministrations, Mrs Lachlan. Kindly permit Nurse Gregory to make her own arrangements for her patient. If she feels Mrs Murray will be better served by the maid then she is quite right to instruct her. I'm sure you have quite enough to do around this place without concerning yourself about the nursing that has to be done.'

'Just so I won't get the blame if anything happens to the mistress while Nurse Gregory is out of the house,' Amena Lachlan said. 'If Deidre has the responsibility then I want it to be known.' She turned and scurried back to her kitchen, waddling like a duck in her hurry to get her short, ample figure out of their sight.

Karen frowned as she left the house with Doctor Sloan. The housekeeper's words stuck in her mind and started a little patch of worry that would not subside, even when she told herself that this was the effect Amena Lachlan wanted. What could possibly happen to

Mrs Murray? Deidre seemed more than capable! The patient was in no danger now from her illness so long as the rules were followed. She tried to enjoy herself, but knew long before the evening was over that the whole thing had been a failure . . .

6

Phelan Sloan did his best to make the evening a success. He had seen how Karen was dejected by loneliness and the strain of just being in Glen Hall. He was angry at the way Amena Lachlan acted towards her, and although he determined to do what he could about the housekeeper's attitude, he knew that Duncan Murray's hands were tied by what had been willed to the housekeeper and her long-suffering husband. He knew that the housekeeper's last words to Karen had upset her, and did what he could to lessen the tension that seemed to encompass them.

They drove to the town of Glen Tay, and Karen was not able to see much of the area before darkness fell, but she was taken up by what did show, and resolved to come again during the day in order to see everything more clearly. They had dinner in the largest hotel, and afterwards went on to a club that made great efforts to compete with those to which she was accustomed in London. She did begin to lose herself in her surroundings, but there was always that niggling thought of her patient in the back of her mind.

Later, when it was time to return to Glen Hall, Karen could not suppress her relief, and they were fairly silent on the return run. Karen had the knowledge that she might have spoiled Sloan's evening by her uneasiness, and when they reached the tall gates of the hall and he stopped the car she turned to him with her mind cluttered with apologies and thanks.

'I'm very sorry about this evening,' she said hesitantly. 'I hope I didn't spoil it for you.'

'How could you have done that?' he countered. 'I took you out to help you along. If you've enjoyed yourself then I'm quite happy. I understand that you're working under a strain here, and mostly because of the housekeeper. I don't think there's much we can do about her, I'm afraid, although I will have a word with Duncan when I call professionally tomorrow.'

'Please don't!' she begged. 'I don't mind Mrs Lachlan. I can put up with her. If I make no complaint I'm sure she'll get tired of her attitude and drop it. On the other hand, if I start complaining she may step up her activities to make me feel uneasy.'

'There's a lot of truth in what you say.' He nodded slowly. 'But this is intolerable! I don't see why you should have to endure it. But I'll hold my tongue for a bit to see if your theory will hold water. It had better or I shall start making trouble! I'm not going to stand by and watch you being treated like that.'

'It doesn't really bother me,' Karen said. 'I concentrate upon Mrs Murray, and nothing else can get through to me.'

'Well I'm glad to hear that, but I

don't like this situation at all. They have no right to drag you into their petty troubles. I don't think any of them are worth worrying over!'

'Then we'll leave it like that, shall we?' Karen half turned to him. 'Thank you for taking the trouble to see that I get a break,' she said. 'It's been very pleasant, Phelan. I have enjoyed this evening. It would have been even better under different circumstances, but I really enjoyed myself.'

'I'm glad! I realize the pressures your work is bringing against you, and it is all so petty, really. There should be no problems at all. But it won't last forever, and soon you'll be able to go on your way. No doubt you've come up against all kinds in your various jobs, haven't you?'

'I have.' Karen smiled as she cast her mind back over some of the cases she had handled. 'Glen Hall isn't so bad, you know. But now I'd better go in.' She glanced at her watch. 'I want to settle Mrs Murray down for the night, and relieve Deidre. She seems a very capable kind of girl, so there was really no need for me to worry about anything.'

'We'll have to go out again, and soon,' he said. 'Let's make a standing date, shall we? I'll arrange my time off to correspond with yours and we'll get out together. You're like a breath of fresh air in my life, Karen, and I'm sure you'll enjoy yourself much better when you're able to get away from the Hall.'

She stared through the gates at the shapeless black pile of the house. A breeze was rustling through the trees and the shadows were dense. One window somewhere in the front of the house was alight, and it beamed at them with stark brilliance, for all the world like the malevolent eye of the mythical Cyclops. She felt a tremor trickle through her, and caught her breath before a sigh could split her lips. She dragged herself from her sombre thoughts and glanced at the silent man by her side, to find his face turned towards her, his pale eyes gleaming in the reflected light coming from the instruments. He nodded as she caught his glance, and his teeth glinted in a smile.

'I won't detain you any longer,' he said. 'I can see that your mind is already in there with your patient. I'll get out to open the gates, and then I'll drive you up to the house.'

He opened his door, but before he could alight there was a movement by the tall iron gates, and Karen caught her breath as she saw a man's figure there. The gates swung open, and then the man came towards the car, and Karen felt a dull throbbing begin in her temples when she recognized him as Roy Murray. He grinned as Phelan Sloan wound down his window.

'I was just making my rounds of the place when I saw your lights and came this way. If you're not going to be long up at the house I'll wait here and close the gates behind you.'

Karen felt the man's eyes upon her despite the fact that he was talking to Sloan.

'I won't be a moment,' the doctor said.

'I'll get out here and walk up to the house,' Karen said. 'I had forgotten that these gates are locked at night.'

'It doesn't matter to me,' Roy Murray remarked. 'I'm in no particular hurry. But I'll see you into the house, Nurse, if you're going to walk.'

'Then I shall see you tomorrow,' the doctor told Karen. 'I'm very happy that you have enjoyed yourself this evening, and later we'll talk about the future.'

'Thank you. You've been most kind.' Karen opened her door and alighted, and Sloan lifted a hand to her and turned his car around. As he drove off a sense of loneliness came to Karen and she stared after the red rear lights of the car. The wind touched her cheek with a cold, invisible hand, and she shivered. Then Roy Murray came to her side, and her nerves tightened as she felt his nearness.

'Have you enjoyed yourself?' he demanded pleasantly.

'It made a change,' she replied, and moved towards the gates, aware that he stayed very close to her side. She halted while he shut the gates, and her nerves seemed to protest against the clash of metal against metal. Then he returned to her side and they began the long walk towards the house.

'I sat with my mother for part of the evening,' he told her in conversational tones. 'You're taking very good care of her, aren't you? She speaks very highly of you.'

'I haven't seen you around since my first day here,' she responded. 'I thought perhaps you had gone away again.'

'No, I've been here. I thought it better to keep out of your way. But I just had to see you this evening.'

She recalled what he had said about falling in love with her, and she could not believe it. How could a man fall in love so swiftly? She was a complete stranger to him. But surely he wouldn't deliberately lie to her! There was no reason for it. She remembered their first moment of meeting, when he had kissed her, and a pang stabbed through her breast. She had liked that kiss despite her shock, and now there was a small but growing sense of desire inside her again, working at her mind, worrying her with its tense insistence.

'Did the doctor kiss you goodnight?' he demanded.

'No!' She answered before she realized what the question was, but then she gasped and half turned to face him. They were standing under tall trees, and the starlight could not penetrate the shadows. She caught the faintest glint in his eyes, but his face was just a pale blur in the night.

'Did I interrupt anything?' he went on. 'I'm sorry if I did. I thought he was waiting for someone to come and open the gates for him.'

'He wouldn't kiss me goodnight,' she said firmly. 'Most gentlemen don't behave that way the first time they meet a girl.'

'That's one in the eye for me!' He

laughed. 'But there can't be any pleasure for a girl out with a man like that. What has he got in his veins, blood or distilled water?'

'I enjoyed my evening with him,' she said quickly.

'No doubt you did, but I can't help thinking that it would have been better if I had taken you out. I know it would have been better for me!'

His hand came out of the darkness and touched her shoulder, and Karen shuddered as if she had received an electric shock. She made no attempt to get away from him, and he paused, halting her in mid-stride.

'I tried to keep away from here this evening,' he told her in low, impassioned tones. 'But you're like a fever in my mind, Karen. I can't control my thoughts any longer. Staying out of your sight around the house has been like a curse upon me. I have the feeling that you could love me, given the chance, and that's why I'm here now.'

She made no reply, and he stepped in

front of her, still holding her arm. She felt as if all her willpower had drained away, and her breathing became laboured. He seemed to tower above her, shapeless and anonymous, and in that staggering moment she could hardly remember what he looked like. But she was keenly aware of her rising emotions, and when his arms slid around her shoulders she made no protest, offered no resistance. He muttered softly to himself as he drew her into his strong embrace, and Karen was surprised by the feeling of security which came over her at their contact.

'I've been waiting all these years for you to come along,' he said in her ear, and then his mouth came sharply against hers, filling her with strange desires and unleashing a flood of hitherto unknown emotions inside her. Passion raged through her and she lifted her arms to his shoulders, pulling herself even closer into his embrace. He raised his head from her for a moment, and she heard him laugh harshly, exultantly, and then the night seemed to close in about them, covering them, concealing everything except their awareness of each other, and Karen closed her eyes and gave herself up to the strange and powerful forces that seemed to encompass them.

She was breathless when he relaxed his embrace, and she tried to catch her breath, but she didn't want him to let her go, and when he tried to step back and attempt to gauge her reception of his act she clung to him with a persistence that came from within. For the first time in her life she was under the control of her emotions.

He laughed harshly and gathered her close once more, and she heard his breathing as a sigh shuddered through him.

'I knew it!' The words were little more than a whisper. 'I could tell, Karen, when I first kissed you. I knew you were meant for me.'

She made no reply, and stood in his embrace like a little girl lost. Nothing outside the small circle of their awareness seemed to matter now, and not even the distant thought of Mrs Murray could rouse her out of the wonderful sense of lethargy that gripped her. Roy kissed her again and again, his passion overflowing and communicating itself to Karen. She was gasping for breath when he finally desisted and moved away, breathless but triumphant.

For some moments she stood motionless, staring at the dark figure of him, and slowly the numbing quality of her desires began to recede. She likened her growing awareness of what had happened to the sensation of coming awake from a very deep sleep, and a series of shudders tore through her, racking her with their intensity. He watched her in silence, immobile now, as though his great passions had left him weak and impotent. Karen took a long breath and moistened her lips, but she didn't know quite what to say.

'You're a most surprising man!' she ventured at length.

'Are you angry at what happened?' He came closer again, and Karen felt her nerves tighten, but he did not touch her.

'No.' She shook her head. 'I'm not angry, and that is what's so surprising about you.'

'You wanted me to do it,' he retorted. 'Even if you didn't know it yourself. It was there deep inside you, and I knew it.'

'How?' she demanded.

'I can't tell. It was just a scrap of knowledge that lay in my mind. I knew you wanted me to kiss you. I knew it would mean something to you, as it meant so much to me.'

Karen suppressed a sigh. He took her arm and she moved towards him, but he checked her and led her on to the house. She walked like a small child being led by a stern adult, and her breast was a rioting playground for many strange emotions that had been given unexpected and complete freedom by his action. She had the strange feeling that she would never be the same again. He had wrought many changes inside her, and some of them were for the better.

Karen was filled with unreality on that walk through the night. The house took shape before them, and the stars were bright, glittering remotely in the dark heavens. Through the nearer trees she saw the thin crescent of a new moon, and some undefinable instinct shivered through her. Some chord had been touched inside her by their contact, and she knew without being told that this man at her side had strange and overwhelming powers against which she could not fight.

But the most surprising thing was that she did not want to fight. He was no longer a stranger! Those moments of physical contact had ripped away her natural reserve. His personality was strong and complete, and she felt weak and pliable in those dark moments as they walked along the drive. She shivered as the last traces of ecstasy seeped away from her, and she would have been eager to return to his arms had he been so inclined. But he was in a hurry to get her into the house, and Karen sensed his apparent confusion. She guessed that he had been similarly affected by their contact, and she was happy with the knowledge.

Yet there was a clear warning sounding in her mind. She drew a deep breath and sighed. She had vowed that neither brother would get close to her because of the trouble that might arise, but here she was feeling on top of the world, and she could not forget that bad trouble had existed between the two men because of a previous nurse at Glen Hall.

But she was only human, and no man had ever aroused such wonderful feelings inside her. She had only guessed at the true meaning of love. Now she had taken a breathless glimpse at it, and she never wanted to go back to the dreariness of before. She glanced at Roy, could sense the fight that was going on inside him, and guessed that he was thinking of the general situation.

What would Duncan do if he learned of that dark incident down among the trees?

When they reached the steps of the house Roy paused and looked down into her face. She tilted her face, half expecting another kiss, and every fibre of her being cried out for it, but he muttered something which she did not catch, and placed his hands upon her shoulders and held her at bay.

'Karen, we'd better forget what happened back there.' His voice was hoarse and unsteady. 'I've been a fool all my life, but this time I've got to make sure nothing goes wrong. There would be too much trouble if I tried to follow my inclinations, but a man is entitled to some happiness, and I know that mine is wrapped up in you. But there are too many problems. I'm sorry if I've aroused you, but it was a moment of madness which I couldn't resist. You've got an important job here, Karen, and I mustn't do anything to jeopardise it.'

She didn't know what to say. There was so much pouring through her brain, but words failed to come to her, and she watched him dumbly, still torn by her half-born desires, but knowing that what she hoped for was wrong. She could not permit her personal life to intrude upon her job. It had happened before to a good many private nurses, and hardly one of them had emerged from the experience without feeling rueful about some aspect of it. He shook her gently.

'I did move you, didn't I?' There was a little triumph in his tones despite the worry that sounded.

'You were not sincere,' she said unsteadily, and her voice sounded strange in her own ears. 'There was another nurse some time ago, wasn't there? Didn't you fall in love with her?'

'No! That wasn't love.' He shook his head. 'But that is over and done with. It's got nothing to do with this.'

'You seem to fall in love very easily.' Now she was trying to find reasons for doubting what he had said, because doubt would strengthen her intention to remain aloof from him and his brother. Her patient needed all the concentration and attention that Karen could muster, and anything less than that would not suffice. 'I must compliment you upon the speed with which you work. You kissed me almost as soon as you set eyes upon me, a complete stranger, and I think that just about sums up the whole situation. You're an accomplished flirt, Roy, and you seem to take great pleasure in arousing a girl and confusing her.'

'It wasn't like that with you,' he muttered.

'I expect you tell that to all the girls.' She was smiling now, but there was a strange sensation of suffocation inside her that was going to be difficult to fight down. 'Well you've had your fun, and it must elate you to know that you can arouse a girl almost against her will.'

'Almost against her will?' he questioned. His teeth glinted for a moment.

'It wasn't against your will. You tried to fight it because you were shocked, but you were in complete agreement all the time. You can't fool me.'

'No matter.' She stepped around him and moved towards the door, and he put a hand upon her arm, their contact sending a flame of emotion through her breast. 'Let's consider the matter closed, shall we?' She paused and stared into his face, unable to see more than a grey blur. 'Let's hope I won't have to go through the same thing with your brother Duncan!'

He gasped at her words, and she regretted them almost immediately, but they were beyond recall, and she knew a retraction would only serve to make them more painful. She turned on her heel and strode into the house, half glancing back to see if he would follow, but he did not, and she closed the door and took a deep breath as she went towards the kitchen. Her mind was filled with conflict. A part of her revelled in the emotions he had aroused inside her, but her saner self was already at work explaining that it was pure madness to hope for progress. There were too many obstacles in the way. She could only force herself to think of the patient and hope that her work would carry her through.

In the kitchen she saw Amena Lachlan and her husband eating supper, and the old lady looked up at her with a curious expression upon her face. She did not speak, however, and Karen swallowed the happy greeting which came automatically to her lips. But Robert Lachlan stared at her, and then spoke slowly.

'Did you have a nice time this evening, Nurse?'

'Very nice, thank you, Mr Lachlan,' she replied, unfreezing a little and smiling. 'Where's Deidre?'

'Up in Mrs Murray's room.' Amena Lachlan spoke heavily, curtly, and her brown eyes glittered as they surveyed Karen.

'There's been no trouble has there?' Karen demanded quickly. Some of her earlier fears returned, and she knew that tension showed in her face. Amena smiled thinly and shook her head.

'Do you think we're not capable of taking care of a sick woman?' she demanded. 'We looked after Mrs Murray when she was really ill!'

Karen nodded and turned to the door, and as she departed the housekeeper called after her.

'Do you want supper, or a hot drink?' she demanded.

'No thank you. I shall settle Mrs Murray down for the night, then go to bed myself.'

'Suit yourself.' Amena Lachlan's voice was harsh and unrelenting.

Karen did not reply, and went up the wide stairs to Mrs Murray's room. She reached the top of the stairs and paused when Duncan Murray appeared from the shadows of the corridor. She was a little startled by his unexpected appearance, and he loomed towards her silently.

'Did you enjoy yourself this evening?'

he demanded in curt tones.

'Yes, thank you,' she replied.

'Was it the doctor's car I saw by the gates some minutes ago?'

'Yes. He left me there and I walked up to the house.'

'Alone in the dark?'

'Why not? There's nothing to fear in the grounds, is there?' She tried to keep the questioning tone out of her voice.

'No, although that damned dog of Roy's is often loose after dark. But you've made friends with it, haven't you?'

'Yes.' She nodded and made a move towards Mrs Murray's room. He reached out a strong hand and seized hold of her arm.

'You didn't come up the drive alone,' he snapped. 'I saw you with Roy.'

'You were spying on me?' she demanded.

'Not spying. I was watching. I know what Roy is. I'm giving you a clear warning. Stay away from him or consider leaving Glen Hall. I want no repetition of the trouble we've already had. I won't repeat this. Stay away from my brother.'

He turned on his heel before Karen could get over her shock, and she watched him striding away along the gloomy corridor. Her thoughts were in a turmoil again, but this time anger mingled with her confusion. She compressed her lips and forced herself to remain calm, but beneath all the surging emotion there was a cold, clear voice telling her that what Duncan said was correct. Trouble was to be avoided. Her duties were clearly defined and she had to stick to them. But his abrupt manner left a bad taste in her mouth, and she couldn't help feeling that the entire evening had been a washout — except, perhaps, for those few moments she had spent on the driveway in Roy Murray's arms, and her cheeks flamed as she recalled them.

7

Mrs Murray continued to show improvement in the days that followed, and Karen found the time to let her feelings settle down again after the gigantic upheaval in her emotions. She didn't see anything at all of Roy Murray in the next four days, although she knew him to be in the house. Duncan seemed to be always bumping into her, and she began to suspect that he planned his movements to correspond with hers, in order to see her often, and she felt that he was spying on her.

Feeling happy about Mrs Murray's progress, Karen threw herself into whole-hearted nursing, and succeeded in driving from her mind some of the doubts which clouded her thoughts. But she could not keep Roy Murray out of her mind, and as each day passed she became aware that her feelings towards him were just a little bit stronger than on the preceding day.

Phelan Sloan made his daily appearance, and now a blossoming friendship appeared between them, based firmly upon that evening that they had spent together, but Karen did not accept his offer for another evening out. She was already too confused by what had happened to her at Roy Murray's hands, and she didn't want to add further complications.

Another week passed, and she was now settled firmly into the household, although the housekeeper did not relax her stern and unfriendly manner. But in every other respect Karen began to feel comfortable. She saw Roy only once during all that time, and that was when he visited his mother in her room. But they didn't even speak, and it shocked Karen to realize that he was unhappy over something. She didn't want to believe it was because of her, but she felt guilty, all the same. For the rest of that day she felt unhappy and lonely, and escaped from the house as the evening turned dark and walked in the grounds, trying to throw off her despair.

A crackling sound in the bushes alerted her, and the next moment Blint appeared like a shadow. The dog whined a little, then dropped at her feet, and Karen bent to fondle its ears. The dog licked her hand and then caught at her sleeve, tugging at her fiercely, and for a heart-stopping moment Karen thought it was turning vicious. She tried to pull away, but the animal's teeth were locked in the fabric of her cardigan, and it dawned upon Karen that the animal was trying to lead her away. She patted the broad head and the animal released its hold upon her, then turned and bounded away along the path that led to the rear of the house. It turned to see if she followed, and Karen hurried after it, filled with wonder at the dog's strange behaviour.

They went past the shed in which the

dog was usually locked at night and Karen blundered along a narrow, overgrown track that went across a paddock and under some trees. It was very dark under the trees and she couldn't see the dog. She paused and called to the animal and it uttered a single bark to guide her. Marvelling at its intelligence, she went on, one hand held before her face to protect it from low branches. She stumbled on the uneven ground and went sprawling. She heard the dog growl once, and hurried up to follow. The animal leapt across a ditch and went thrusting through a tall, thin hedge, and Karen was breathless as she went on. She found herself outside the immediate grounds of the Hall, and paused to take stock of her bearings.

Open ground stretched away into the shadows, and she could not see to any great distance. Blint halted and turned to face her, tongue lolling from his mouth, his head hanging low. She peered closely at the animal, seeing with great difficulty that it was in distress, and her mind began to quest for an explanation of its strange behaviour. It couldn't have asked more plainly for her company if it had been endowed with human speech, and Karen suddenly felt a pang of fear. Had the dog been out with Roy this afternoon? Was Roy in some kind of trouble now and needing help? Had he sent the animal to fetch someone from the house?

At first she dismissed the thought as sheer nonsense, but the dog came at her again and tried to seize hold of her sleeve. She patted his head and spoke gently to him.

'Take it easy, Blint. If Roy is out there on the moors and in need of help then I can't do anything on my own. I'm not equipped for a rescue hunt. We'll have to go back to the house for help.'

She turned to hurry back along the route she had covered and the dog came at her several times, attempting to turn her back in the original direction. She patted his head and tried to reassure him, and the very fact that he was upset seemed to prove to her that something was amiss and that it affected his master.

She was breathless as she hurried to the kitchen door of the great house, and she stumbled inside with the dog following her. Amena Lachlan uttered a curse and sprang to her feet at the sight of the dog.

'Get him out of here!' the woman shouted. 'I won't have that great brute in the house.'

Karen shook her head impatiently and blurted out the facts of her fears, and she saw a cunning glitter come into the housekeeper's dark eyes, but Robert Lachlan, seated in his favourite corner with a newspaper, looked up quickly and stared at her.

'Roy was out on the moors this morning with the dog,' he said. 'I haven't seen him come back.'

He got to his feet and approached the dog, bending to examine the animal. Then he looked up at Karen and his wrinkled face was tense with concern.

'I think something has happened to Roy out there,' Karen said firmly. 'We'd better inform Duncan and get a search party organized. He may be lying hurt somewhere.'

'Not Roy Murray!' Amena Lachlan shook her head firmly. 'He knows the moors better than most men in these parts. The Devil takes care of his own! He'll be all right.'

'I'll get lanterns and a rope,' Robert Lachlan said, starting to the back door. 'Better keep the dog in here until we're ready to leave. Perhaps you'll warn Duncan, Nurse Gregory.'

Karen didn't hesitate, but hurried through to the hall and on into the library. But there was no sign of Duncan, and she stood for a moment in the doorway, staring around the hall, wondering where Duncan could be. Then Deidre came out of the front lounge, and the girl smiled as she walked towards Karen.

'Enjoy your stroll in the gardens?' she demanded.

'I was enjoying it until the dog came

for me,' Karen said. She explained what had happened and asked for Duncan Murray.

'But he's not in the house,' the maid said. 'I haven't seen him since early afternoon. He went out to do some checking on the estate farms, and he told me he wouldn't be back until late.'

'What about Roy?' Karen demanded. 'Did you see him at all?'

'He went out with Blint early in the morning, but he never tells anyone where he goes!'

Karen hurried back to the kitchen, to find Amena feeding the dog, but the animal was clearly uneasy and wanted to get back out to the moors. It was obvious the animal was concerned about something, and to Karen's mind it could only be it's master's welfare that was bothering it.

Robert Lachlan looked in at the doorway and enquired after Duncan, and he shook his head when Karen reported that the elder brother was not in the house.

'I'll come with you,' she said fearfully. 'If something has happened to him I'll be able to give first aid. But perhaps it would be possible for someone to ring around the farms on the estate asking for Duncan. He should have warning of this.'

'I'll do it,' Amena Lachlan said, and there was a softer note in her tones. She eyed Karen for a moment. 'It is right that you should go along with my husband in case Roy is lying injured out there, but you cannot go dressed as you are. Put on a thick coat and some stout shoes.'

'I won't be a moment.' Karen hurried to the door and raced up to her room, pausing to warn Deidre, who was standing in the hall, to stand by with Mrs Murray until she returned. She changed in great haste and went breathlessly back to the kitchen, where Robert Lachlan was waiting and ready to go. He had the dog on a leash now, and the animal was whining and scratching at the kitchen door, its eyes piteous with concern.

Karen suppressed a shiver as they went out into the night, and the swinging lantern in Robert Lachlan's hand cast indistinct rays across the shadows, distorting them as it pressed back the blackness. The big dog almost dragged the old man along, and Karen was half-running to keep abreast of them. Soon they were out on the open moor, and the lantern-light was puny and almost ineffective against the wide stretch of black sky.

How long they trudged along Karen did not know, but her legs were aching by the time the dog paused and cast around, using its instincts to find the spot it had intended getting them to. They were beneath a high ridge, and great boulders lay ominously shadowed in the near darkness. Karen could sense rather than see them, and she could feel a tingling along her spine as she gazed fearfully around. She felt so lonely, dwarfed by the elementary forces of Nature which surrounded her. Robert

Lachlan startled her by suddenly calling out in long-drawn tones that echoed eerily through the shadows. They listened intently when he fell silent, but only the moaning of the wind came to their ears, and in that simple sound there was an edge of hostility.

The dog suddenly pulled to the right, and they followed eagerly, the dancing rays of the lantern touching the ground obliquely, throwing up its own pattern of shadows to confuse their eyes, and Karen had the feeling that they had been searching for a lifetime and were condemned to go on through eternity with these fruitless efforts. But Blint suddenly raced forward, growling and whining, and as they followed swiftly Karen saw the figure of a man stretched out upon the ground, lying beside a large rock which had evidently plunged down from the ridge high above.

Karen seemed to freeze inside as she spotted the figure, and she felt her heart lurch in sudden fear. Roy! The name flashed through her mind in big letters and she hurried forward and flung herself to her knees beside the body. Robert Lachlan stood over her with the lantern held high, and Karen's hands were trembling as she reached out and tugged at the shoulders of the unconscious man, pulling him gently over on to his back. She gasped with mingled shock and relief when she saw Duncan Murray's features in the lantern-light, and her first thought was that this was not Roy! Then her personal self faded and her professional instincts took over.

Duncan Murray was unconscious, and there was a smear of blood on his forehead, half concealing a large bruise. Karen went to work on him, checking for broken ribs and limbs, and was relieved to discover that his only injury seemed to be the head wound. She looked up at the silent Robert Lachlan.

'He mustn't be moved,' she said quickly. 'Give me that blanket you've brought. Then you'd better go back and arrange for an ambulance to be brought here. He'll have to go to hospital. It seems to me that his skull has suffered a fracture.'

The gardener nodded grimly, and unfolded the blanket he had brought. Karen wrapped it around the motionless figure, instinctively glancing at her watch. The dog settled down at her side, and she wondered that the animal, which seemed to belong to Roy, had taken to guarding Duncan.

'I'll leave you the lantern,' the old man said. 'I can find my way back to the Hall in the dark. But will you be all right here until I get back?'

'I'll be all right.' Karen nodded as she reached out and patted the big dog. 'Blint will take care of us. But hurry, Mr Lachlan. Duncan seems to be very seriously hurt.'

'I shan't have to go all the way back to the Hall,' he said, evidently thinking hard. 'There's a telephone box on the road not far from here, and it will be quicker for me to use that. I can make an emergency call and direct them to the telephone box, then bring them the rest of the way myself. They'd never find this spot just from my directions. You have to live here in order to know the moors.'

'Hurry,' Karen urged him. 'Be as quick as you can. Perhaps you'd better call Doctor Sloan. He might be able to get here sooner than the ambulance from town.'

'I'll do the best I can,' Robert Lachlan said, and turned and hurried away into the darkness.

Karen huddled herself beside the unconscious man and drew the lantern close. The night was cold, the wind spiteful, and she was thankful that she had put on her thick coat. But she had forgotten her gloves and her hands were cold. She called the dog closer, and Blint lumped himself down beside her and dropped his large head into her lap. She could feel his warmth under her hands, and rubbed his ears gratefully.

It was eerie sitting within the circle of lantern-light, with deep darkness pressing in all around. The stars were bright overhead, and far to the east a faint crescent of the moon showed in silver light. But Karen had little time to stare at the beauties of Nature. She was concerned about Duncan Murray. How long had the man lain here unconscious? How had he been injured? It didn't seem feasible to her that the large rock almost at his side had been the cause of his condition. If it had tumbled down from the top of the ridge the force of it would have killed him instantly. The dog, too! What was it doing here with Duncan? If Roy had gone out on the moors the dog would have accompanied him! She thought about Roy, and a sudden pang touched her breast as her intuition worked. Had Roy and Duncan met out here? She shivered as she considered, and tried to cast the thought aside. She turned her attention once again to the injured man, but there was nothing she could do for him except keep him warm.

How long she waited she did not check, but it seemed an eternity before the dog growled deep in its throat. Karen stirred and peered around intently. A moment later she caught sight of car headlights, and she pushed herself stiffly to her feet and lifted the lantern to wave it. A few minutes later Phelan Sloan's car came to a halt nearby.

Sloan alighted from the car with his medical bag in his hand, and Blint went forward to greet him. Karen sighed heavily. She was half frozen, but that fact worried her only because she was afraid that exposure might have worked its insidious way into Duncan's system.

'Karen, are you all right?' Sloan demanded as he came level and dropped to his knees beside the unconscious man.

'I'm all right,' she responded. 'But I'm afraid Duncan is in a poor way. I've checked him for broken ribs and limbs and he's all right that way, but I suspect he's got a fractured skull.'

'You're right!' Sloan's deft fingers gently probed the injury. 'There's a slight indentation here. Must have been hit by a falling rock, but one would expect a man of his experience to avoid an obvious danger like that.' He paused and carried out a swift examination. 'It seems to be his only injury, but that's bad enough. He's in deep shock, and no doubt he's beginning to suffer from exposure. It was a good thought of yours to bring a blanket with you. Tell me what really happened.'

He prepared and administered an injection as Karen related the events, and he nodded from time to time.

'I'll inform the police when Duncan has been taken to hospital,' he retorted.

'The police!' Karen could not keep the surprise from her tones. 'But this was an accident.'

'It will have to be reported all the same.' He smiled at her. 'You don't understand the half of what has been happening around here, Karen. I don't suppose anyone at the Hall told you that Duncan's life had been threatened.'

'No!' she gasped, and her eyes widened. 'By whom?'

'I wouldn't know. I've just had the gossip of it to go by, but why do you think they keep such a fierce dog in the grounds?'

'Blint isn't fierce!' she protested.

'Not to friends, of course, but I wouldn't want to walk through the grounds at night when he's loose.'

'Roy told me he's never loose at night.'

'That's what they told me when I first started calling, but when there was an emergency over Mrs Murray one night they forgot to get the dog in, and he almost had me when I pulled up at the gates to let myself into the grounds.'

'Roy was on hand to let me in that evening we went out together,' Karen said slowly. 'I don't like the sound of all this, Phelan. What do you suppose is happening?'

'I wouldn't even try to hazard a guess,' he retorted, shaking his head, and his face was grim and drawn in the dim lantern-light. 'I ought not say, but I can't help feeling that the only trouble at Glen Hall is between Roy and Duncan.'

'You don't think Roy had anything to do with Duncan's accident, do you?' There was a tinge of horror in Karen's tones, and Sloan studied her face for a moment.

'You're falling in love with Roy, aren't you, Karen?' he demanded slowly.

'In love!' She stared at him, shaking her head slowly, her face showing surprise at his words, and he would never forget the regret which came to him in that moment. 'No!' She spoke the word fiercely, as if trying to convince herself that she spoke the truth. 'You're quite wrong, Phelan.'

'Now isn't the time to talk about such matters, but I would warn you to be very careful, Karen. I did mention what happened during the stay of the previous nurse. It would be dreadful if the same sort of situation arose, because next time I'm sure there would be murder done at Glen Hall. I don't know how it was avoided the last time.'

'Who was to blame for it?' she questioned, and there seemed to be a breathlessness inside her that stifled.

'That's anyone's guess. I think the girl was out to better herself in any way she could. She made a play for Roy, and at first he wasn't interested, but when he began to show interest it awakened something in Duncan, and no doubt the girl thought Duncan was a better catch, he being the eldest son, and she turned her attentions to him. Putting myself in Roy's place, I must say that I wouldn't have stood for what happened.'

'So Roy wasn't to blame for that particular situation!' Karen didn't know why she should feel so relieved. She suppressed a sigh and got to her feet to pace silently to and fro. She was cold, and her legs were stiff and frozen. But she didn't dwell upon her discomforts. Her mind was too busy working over what Phelan had said. Love! She shook her head. She wasn't in love with Roy Murray! She wasn't in love with anyone! She took a deep breath and paused to stare into the night, looking for the headlamps of the ambulance, but the shadows were impenetrable and she saw and heard nothing.

There was an unsettled feeling growing up in her mind. She was aware of it although she tried to ignore the fact, and she couldn't tell what had activated it. She had never been fully in love before in her life, although one painful episode had at the time made her think that she had been. Now she knew differently, and she was afraid that the uneasiness inside her breast was the start of something that might prove awkward. She couldn't face her duty with personal worries clouding her judgment and her work. It was good practice to keep her private life away from duty, and as far removed as possible. She pictured Roy's face, and an undefinable pang stabbed her deeply. Then she turned and looked at the motionless figure lying on the ground, blanket-covered and unconscious, and she wondered what had happened here to cause this particular situation. Did Roy have a hand in his brother's accident?

Sloan came to her side, gently touching her arm to gain her attention. She looked at him quickly, startled by his interruption. Her thoughts had been running deeply into her subconscious mind, and she felt like someone being awakened from heavy slumber as she gazed at him with widening blue eyes.

'Why don't you go and sit in the car?' he demanded. 'You're half frozen. There's nothing you can do out here. The ambulance won't be long now, and then I'll be able to drive you home.'

'I'm all right,' she said softly. 'I'm not feeling the cold. I'll stay here.'

He nodded, realizing that she wanted to think over what had happened, and he went back to the unconscious Duncan. Karen watched him, her thoughts quickening again, and she remained thoughtful until the first sounds of an engine reached her ears. Then she turned, and spotted the approaching headlamps of a vehicle. It came up rapidly and proved to be the ambulance, and Robert Lachlan jumped to the ground as it halted.

It was the work of moments for the ambulancemen to transfer Duncan to their vehicle, and then the ambulance started back the way it had come. Phelan Sloan took Karen's arm and led her towards the car, and Lachlan collected his lantern and called to the dog. They got into Sloan's car and drove in silence back to the Hall, and as they neared the edge of the moors Karen could feel a protest welling up inside her. She wouldn't believe that Roy had anything to do with his brother's injuries. She had the feeling that he could not possibly do such a cowardly and brutal thing, but she was afraid to face the facts. Somehow, there was a dark worry in her mind, stretching like black thread across the line of her thoughts, and it seemed insurmountable and so terribly unreal. That seemed to be the most difficult thing for her to accomplish, but it had to be done. She must decide which was fantasy and which was real.

Deep inside her she wanted to believe that Roy was incapable of wrong, and that gave rise to conjecture. She considered Sloan's words. Was she in love with Roy? Had the doctor seen something about her which indicated her subconscious desires? She had no way of knowing, and it troubled her greatly. In this moment of indecision and worry she could only hope, and that was what she was doing as Sloan drove off the moors . . .

8

Lachlan took away Blint to lock him in the shed as soon as they reached Glen Hall, and Sloan escorted Karen into the house. She was shivering as they crossed the threshold, and the doctor studied her face for a moment.

'Better take a hot bath and then come down to the kitchen for a drink,' he suggested. 'I'll have a talk to the staff, and see if Roy is here. We'd better keep the news of what has happened from Mrs Murray until we know the extent of Duncan's injuries. I shall stay here for a bit, so don't worry about anything.'

Karen nodded. She felt strangely indecisive. Deidre appeared on the stairs, and came hurrying down to greet them.

'Mrs Murray has been asking for you, Karen,' the maid said. 'She's restless tonight, and keeps wanting to see Roy or Duncan. I've told her they're both out at the moment, and she wants to see them as soon as they return.'

'I'll go and change, then see her,' Karen said.

'Don't forget to come for that drink,' Sloan said. 'We don't want you cracking up, do we?' His smile was warm and friendly, and Karen felt some of his cheerfulness reflect upon her. She nodded as she hurried up the stairs.

After taking a shower and changing, she went into the sick room, but Mrs Murray was asleep, and Karen sighed with relief and tiptoed out. She went down to the kitchen, to find Sloan and Lachlan discussing the accident. Amena Lachlan got to her feet from the big chair that her husband always favoured, and brought Karen a hot drink. The woman's lined face was gentle now, and Karen felt a sudden ray of hope that what had happened this evening had finally mellowed the housekeeper.

'How are you feeling now?' Phelan

Sloan demanded, getting to his feet.

'Much better,' Karen replied thankfully. 'I didn't think I could get so cold out there. It's hardly the end of summer, and yet it's possible to freeze to death on those moors.'

'That's a sad fact that many visitors never learn until it is almost too late,' Robert Lachlan said. He was friendly now, his last reserve gone, and Karen realized that the incident on the moors had drawn them closer together. She was being accepted. It pleased her, but the fact was almost lost beneath the layers of worry that gripped her.

'I'll telephone the hospital now,' Sloan said. 'They've had time to examine Duncan.'

'Isn't Roy home yet?' Karen demanded as the doctor left the room.

'Not yet.' Deidre spoke from the corner, and the girl's dark eyes showed worry as she met Karen's paler gaze.

'Does anyone know where he went?' Karen pursued.

'That one never tells,' Amena said

heavily, and her tones showed a little respect, Karen noticed.

'Surely you know where he spends his time, or part of it,' Karen went on. 'It's imperative that we find him.'

'He'll come back in his own good time,' Robert Lachlan said heavily.

'What do you think happened to Duncan?' Karen asked him, and the old Scot shook his grizzled head.

'It was an accident, and it happens all too frequently to people on the moors,' he said emphatically.

'Duncan should have known better,' Amena added, and she stared at Karen with truculence showing in her eyes.

'I thought Blint was Roy's dog.' Karen kept her tones even and non-committal.

'So he is, but Duncan has a way with animals, and if Roy never took that dog for exercise then Duncan himself attended to the chore.' Robert Lachlan moved to his favourite chair and dropped heavily into it. Amena fetched his slippers and helped him get out of his boots.

'Did you look in on Mrs Murray?'

Deidre asked Karen.

'She's asleep now,' Karen said. 'Did Doctor Sloan mention that no word of this must be mentioned to Mrs Murray?'

'Aye, it'll be wise to keep it from her,' Lachlan said. 'It will do to tell her that Duncan has gone over to Gillieburn for a few days on business. He's sometimes over there for a week at a time.'

Karen nodded. 'I'll remember that,' she said. 'But I wish we could contact Roy.'

The kitchen door opened and Sloan entered. He paused to look around at their intent faces, then moved to Karen's side, and she had the feeling that his news was not so good.

'They're performing an emergency operation on Duncan,' he said slowly. 'It will be some time before we know the result, but his chances are about fifty-fifty.'

'He might die?' Amena demanded in great agitation.

'That's certainly possible. A lot

would depend upon his general condition of health. But the injury was a bad one, and we don't know how long he lay out there after being struck.'

'I wish Roy would return,' Karen said worriedly.

'I also rang the police, and Constable Snell will be along shortly to take statements.' Phelan Sloan shook his head as he went to sit down at the long table. He looked at Karen, and she didn't like the worry that showed upon his face.

Where was Roy? Karen could not keep his name from her mind. She felt as if she were descending into a nightmarish pit of fear. The very fact that Duncan was now fighting for his life was outweighed by the knowledge that her intuition blamed Roy for what had happened to his brother. But she was being ridiculous, she tried to tell herself. Roy was not the type to harm anyone. She knew that instinctively, as if he had proved it to her time and again.

The evening wore away relentlessly, and there was no lessening of the worry that filled Karen. The local constable arrived and took statements. Karen's was a relatively simple work, and there were no extra questions for her, but she tensed when the constable enquired after Roy, and no-one could tell him anything.

'I'll call back later to talk with him,' the policeman said, putting away his notebook. 'If he comes in sooner, get him to telephone me, will you?'

They nodded, and Deidre saw him out. Karen noticed the tension in the kitchen afterwards, and wanted to go to the privacy of her room, but she did not because she was afraid to be alone with her nagging thoughts. She went up to Mrs Murray later, and settled the woman for the night, avoiding the woman's questions about the whereabouts of her sons. Mrs Murray seemed to sense that something was wrong, and it needed all of Karen's skill to avoid being cornered by questions.

'It's not like Duncan to go away for a few days without first telling me about it,' Mrs Murray said wonderingly.

'I think it was something that came up unexpectedly,' Karen said. 'He didn't think he would be away more than an hour or two, but then discovered his presence was needed for much longer, and he telephoned to say he wouldn't be coming home tonight.' As she spoke, Karen mentally kept her fingers crossed, and she prayed that it would not be her painful duty later to tell this woman that her eldest son was dead! She was quite relieved when Mrs Murray settled down and drifted into sleep, and she couldn't get back to the kitchen quickly enough to check if Roy had come in.

Amena Lachlan had gone to bed, but Deidre still sat up, and Karen joined the girl.

'Doctor Sloan had to go,' the maid said. 'There was a call for him. He had left a message that he would be here, but he said he would be back as soon as possible.'

'He's been a great help this evening,' Karen said, 'but there isn't much he can do now. Did he say anything about ringing the hospital again for a report of Duncan's condition?'

'He said to give them another half hour at least,' Deidre said. She eyed Karen speculatively, and saw something of the distress that gripped Karen. 'What do you think happened, Karen?' she demanded.

'I don't know. I would give a lot to find out.' Karen stared into the girl's questioning face. 'Anything could have happened, I suppose.'

'Duncan isn't the kind of man to take any risks,' the girl asserted. 'He was an experienced man, and wouldn't make the elementary mistake of walking under a dangerous ridge.'

'So what do you think happened?' Karen pursued.

'I think he met Roy out there, either by appointment or by accident.'

'Or they might have met because one wanted to see the other,' Karen almost whispered.

'You think one followed the other out

and attacked him without warning?' There was shock showing in Deidre's brown eyes.

'You mean Roy, of course!' Karen compressed her lips and shook her head. 'I don't know him very well, but I don't think he's the kind of man to do a thing like that.'

'He's been pushed almost to the brink of violence before,' Deidre said. 'Don't think I'm on Duncan's side, because I'm not. But Roy has been provoked beyond human restraint. Now that you have entered the situation it must have been like the last straw.'

'Me!' Karen shook her head in wonder. 'How do I get into this?'

'It's like history repeating itself.' The girl spoke seriously, a frown upon her face. 'I heard Duncan warning Roy to stay away from you.'

'When was this?' Karen was startled by the knowledge.

'Two or three days ago.'

'What did Roy reply to that?' There was a breathlessness in Karen which she could not overcome.

'He told Duncan to mind his own business. I heard him say that the other time didn't matter, because he hadn't loved the girl. Bu you were different, and he wouldn't stand for any interference whatever.'

'I've done all I could not to get caught up in anything,' Karen said softly, and there was agony in her mind. If she were to blame for this then she would never be able to live it down, no matter the circumstances.

'It certainly wasn't your fault,' Deidre told her consolingly. 'I don't know how any man could refrain from falling in love with you.'

The telephone rang and Deidre hurried out of the kitchen to answer it. Karen stared at Robert Lachlan, who sat dozing in his favourite chair. She thought she saw his eyelids flicker, but couldn't be sure. He made no move, and if he was awake then he obviously didn't want to talk. She turned on her heel and left the kitchen, intending to go into the library or the front lounge, but Deidre stopped her in the hall.

'That was the hospital,' the girl said. 'Duncan's had the operation and he's as well as can be expected. They say to call again first thing in the morning, but they will ring us if his condition gives cause for alarm.'

'So he's got a good chance now!' Karen swayed as relief sped through her. 'When he recovers consciousness he'll be able to tell what happened.'

'I hope for everyone's sake that it was an accident.' Deidre stared at Karen, and for a moment there was silence between them. Then Karen nodded.

'I shall pray for that to be so,' she said. 'I'm going to bed now, Deidre. I have my duties tomorrow to attend to, and Mrs Murray may be restless tonight.'

'I hope you won't have any trouble with her,' the maid said. 'You could do with a good night's sleep yourself. You look worn out.'

'It's been a worrying evening.' Karen

smiled thinly and went on up the stairs to her room. She paused and looked down at the maid. 'If Doctor Sloan returns tell him I've gone to bed, will you?' she demanded.

'Leave it to me, because I shall be up for a long time yet,' Deidre told her.

Karen went to check her patient, and found Mrs Murray in a deep, natural sleep, and she sighed her relief as she went into her own room and prepared to go to bed. When she lay in the darkness her worst fears were realized, and she lay awake with her mind throbbing with conjecture. She relived those tense minutes when she had been alone on the moors with an unconscious Duncan, and she could not keep Roy's name out of the forefront of her thoughts. She dared not take a sleeping tablet for fear that Mrs Murray might want her during the night, and she closed her eyes and used all manner of tricks to get her mind to relax. But nothing seemed to work. She consigned herself to lying awake for hours, and without knowing it, drifted silently and gently into sleep. It was morning when she suddenly opened her eyes, and bright sunlight lay in the room and across the curtained window. She sat up as her mind refilled with all the worries that had beset her the evening before, and she leaped out of bed and hurriedly slipped into her dressing gown.

Her first thought was for her patient, and she tiptoed into Mrs Murray's room. The woman was still asleep, and Karen nodded gratefully. The longer she could postpone talking about Duncan the better. She went into the bathroom and took a shower, then dressed and went down to the kitchen, wondering what sort of news awaited her. She found Amena and Deidre there, and Deidre looked as if she had been up all night. The housekeeper greeted Karen, but in her usual distant way.

'Have you rung the hospital this morning?' Karen demanded.

'Not yet. I thought you would do it,' Deidre replied.

'I'll do it now.' Karen turned to the

door, and there she paused. 'Did Roy come home last night?'

'I didn't see him,' the maid replied, 'and I looked in his room a few minutes ago and the bed hasn't been slept in.'

Karen caught Amena's eye, and the old lady pulled a wry face.

'It often happens,' she said. 'But if he doesn't sleep in the house then he's probably in the cabin above Monderbie.'

'I never thought of that,' Deidre said. 'I expect that's where he is. That would be why Duncan was exercising the dog on the moor. He always does that when he knows Roy won't be home.'

'Is there a telephone in the cabin?' Karen demanded.

'No.' Amena Lachlan shook her head and turned to the stove. 'But you better ring the hospital now and let us know the worst.'

'They would have rung if his condition gave cause for alarm,' Karen said. She left the kitchen and walked across the hall, and the telephone rang just before she reached it. The shrill sound grated against her nerves and she hurried forward and snatched up the reciever. Almost at once, Phelan Sloan spoke in her ear.

'Karen,' he said after she gave the number. 'Have you rung the hospital this morning?'

'Not yet. I was about to do so when you called.'

'I've just been through to them, and Duncan is comfortable this morning, although he hasn't regained consciousness yet. Did Roy come home?'

'No. I've just learned that he may have stayed the night in a cabin above Monderbie.'

'I know the place. Is someone going over there to find out?'

'There's no-one here able to go,' Karen said. 'Where is the place?'

'Can you drive?' Sloan countered.

'Yes, and I have a current licence to do so.' Karen smiled slowly. 'I expect there is a car here, so if I ask directions I could drive over there myself.'

'Deidre will give you directions,' he said. 'Karen, I'd like to see you some time today.'

'I shall be here all the time today,' she retorted.

'Then we'll arrange for a talk when I've seen Mrs Murray. I have a lot to do today, so it will be well into the afternoon before I get around to visiting the Hall.'

'I shall look out for you,' Karen retorted.

He hung up and she went back into the kitchen to report on Duncan's condition. She saw relief come to Deidre's face, but Amena shrugged and went on with her work.

'If you'll prepare Mrs Murray's breakfast and attend to her I'll take the car and go to the cabin to look for Roy,' Karen said to Deidre. 'Is it far from here?'

'About five miles, and if you follow the moors road you can't miss it,' Deidre said. 'I wish you would go, Karen. It will be better if Roy knows about the accident. His place is here now.'

'He won't want anything to do with the estate,' Amena said heavily. 'Better to let him idle away his time. The estate has never had any room for him before.'

'But if Duncan isn't able to run the affairs for some time then it's Roy's duty to step into the breach,' the maid pointed out.

'I'll try to find him,' Karen said. 'Perhaps I'd better have some breakfast before setting out. Deidre, you'll have to try and put Mrs Murray off if she asks about either of her sons.'

'She knows the arrangement that if one isn't here then the other is,' Amena said thinly. 'If you can't produce either of them then she'll know there's something wrong.'

'Do what you can, anyway,' Karen said, and the maid nodded.

Amena Lachlan produced breakfast for Karen, who ate quickly, and Deidre came to her side and gave her directions for finding the cabin above

Monderbie. Karen repeated the girl's words and memorized them. She was anxious to be off, but ate enough to stay her through the morning. Deidre went with her out to the garages, and Karen selected a shooting brake and got behind the wheel. There was a full tank of petrol, and she started up and drove the car around the house, familiarizing herself with the controls. Then she drove away, and discovered the road over the moors, and found herself heading towards the distant mountains.

The morning was bright and clear, with a few patches of mist showing across the moors. But it was the kind of day one could wish for a holiday, and it didn't seem fair to Karen that such natural glory should have its sharpness dulled for her by the worries circulating her mind.

The ground began to rise and the road followed the contours of the countryside. Karen felt her heart lighten imperceptibly, but she could not maintain her elation. There were too many nagging doubts in her mind. Soon she saw the brightness of water ahead and to the right, and she guessed that the loch Deidre had mentioned was nearby. Then the narrow road took a sharp turning to the right and she halted by a fork. A tall signpost showed the way, and Karen went on, beginning to feel the first spasms of tension flooding her as she looked forward to seeing Roy.

Doctor Sloan's words came to her as she drove on. Was she in love with Roy? It didn't seem possible, but there were strange stirrings inside her, and when she recalled the way Roy had kissed her she knew something strange and unusual had happened inside her. But worry kept most of her mental attitudes under a blanket of shock, and she drove on and on, wanting to see Roy again but afraid of what he might have to tell her when they met.

The road twisted and lifted until it was high above the loch and she could see to a great distance. In circumstances other than the present she would have been thrilled by the scenery, but she set her teeth and compressed her lips as she went on. One day, she half promised herself, she would come back and take full enjoyment from all of this!

Then she saw the cabin. It was just as Deidre had described it, perched alone on a crag overlooking the water, and Karen could not wonder that it was Roy's favourite spot. She sent the car up the last incline and braked sharply in front of the little cabin, switching off the engine and letting silence rush in about her from all sides. For a moment she sat there staring at the front of the building, hoping against hope that Roy was here, and then she opened the car door and alighted, to stand beside the vehicle and let her gaze wander slowly and photographically across the panorama awaiting her. She heaved a long, emotional sigh as the beauty of the spot tore into her, and longing filled her, an intangible desire that was buried deep in her subconscious mind so that even she did not know exactly what it was she wanted. But hope welled up from its inexhaustible spring in her breast, and she dragged her mind back to the present and shook herself free from the reverie.

'Like what you see?' a voice called to her, and she lifted her eyes to see Roy standing in the cabin doorway. There was a grin on his face, and pleasurable surprise. He came towards her when she looked at him, and now there was a frown replacing his pleasure. 'What brings you up here, Karen?' he demanded in suddenly sharper tones. 'There's nothing the matter with Mother, is there?'

'No, it isn't your mother, Roy,' she explained quickly, and told him what had happened the previous evening. She watched his face for expression, wondering if she would see guilt or fear, but his features were inscrutible, and at her words he frowned slightly and reached out to take hold of her hands.

'You say he's comfortable this morning?' he demanded.

'Yes. That means he's got a good chance of recovering.'

'I wonder what happened to him!' He frowned, staring down into her worried face. 'Thank you for taking care of him, Karen. That wasn't in your line of duty.'

'But it was, Roy,' she said quickly. 'It is one's duty to do all that's possible for someone hurt or sick, whether one is a professional nurse or not.'

'That's your philosophy!' He smiled, looking the outdoor type in an open-neck red check shirt. The sleeves were rolled to the elbows, revealing strong, muscular arms. 'A lot of people, especially around here, don't subscribe to such sentiments. You've seen what they're like in the Hall. Take Amena for instance. There isn't a scrap of emotion in her. She's a sub-human woman. No wonder she and Robert never had any romance.' He paused and sighed heavily. 'I suppose I'd better come back to the Hall with you. This has been kept from Mother, hasn't it?'

'Yes. She thinks Duncan has gone somewhere on business. I hope she won't miss him too much, and that's why I came for you. If you're at the Hall she won't ask too many questions.'

Karen was watching his face closely as she spoke, and there was an undefinable thrill wending its way through her breast. She could feel something akin to love rearing its head inside her, and wondered at it and at herself, for she had no inclination to subdue it. Was she coming under his spell? He had personality and magnetism, and she felt weak and indecisive as she considered him. But he had undermined her rigid rule of not fraternizing with the male relatives of her patients. He had kissed her in the very first moment of their meeting, and perhaps he had known that such a kiss would have some effect upon her, no matter how long it took to mature.

'What are you thinking, Karen?' he

asked, and she realized that he was watching her closely. 'If I didn't know better I would say that you're falling in love with me!' His voice was rough and unsteady, and she caught her breath as he took a step towards her and opened his arms.

'No,' she said weakly. 'We must get back to the Hall. Your brother is desperately ill, Roy. You'll have to go to the hospital.'

'He wouldn't do that if I were in his place,' he said harshly, and now his voice was like a stranger's, thin and brittle, as if ready to snap under the strain of the emotions rising within him.

'Two wrongs never made a right,' she quoted, and saw him smile slowly.

'I have no intention of doing what Duncan would do in the circumstances,' he told her softly. 'I'm not as black as I've been painted, Karen, and I'm improving all the time. But before we go you can give me a few moments. You've come all this way to find me and

I want to reward you.' He smiled gently. 'Don't deny it, but I can tell that you would find ample reward in a kiss.'

She made no move when he took her gently into his strong arms, but she quivered as their lips touched. A great relief seemed to well up inside her and she closed her eyes and relaxed into ecstasy. It was in that wonderful moment when the truth struck her powerfully. She was in love with him!

9

The ensuing days were filled with tension for Karen as she carried out her duties around the Hall. It was a blessing that Mrs Murray seemed to gain strength all the time, but Duncan lay in a coma at the hospital, and had not regained consciousness since he'd suffered the accident. Roy was always around, Karen discovered, and he spent a lot of time with his mother. But he was putting on a bold front, Karen could tell, and sometimes, when he didn't know he was under observation, she noticed the agony in his face and eyes.

Her feelings for him solidified as the days went by, despite the worries that occupied her mind, for she could not get rid of the thought that Roy might have been involved in his brother's accident. When she saw his uneasiness she put it down to fear that Duncan would tell the truth when he recovered, for she could not bring herself to believe that love and regard existed between the two men. Whatever had happened between them in the past, it must have been heavy with impact, because neither of them seemed to have the desire to forget it.

Roy seemed to avoid her, she slowly discovered. He didn't mind talking to her in the company of someone else, but when they were alone at any time he soon made excuses for leaving her, and she began to think that he was afraid she had guessed the truth and wanted to question him about it. Karen became so sensitive upon this point that one evening when she found him alone in the library, seated at the desk and trying to do Duncan's work, she prevented him from leaving the room and slipped into his arms.

'Don't go, Roy,' she pleaded softly. 'I must talk to you.'

'I'm busy at the moment,' he replied,

trying to disengage himself, but she clung to him with all her strength, and although he began to fight her he soon relaxed and gave in. 'What's on your mind?' he demanded.

'You've been so different since we came back from that cabin,' she said. 'I've been watching you when you weren't aware of the fact, and I'm certain there's something more than the general situation worrying you.'

He looked down into her intent face, saw that her only desire was to help him in any way she could and he smiled slowly and bent his head to kiss her on the lips.

'You're a discerning girl,' he said, nodding. 'But I've been trying to act sensibly, that's all. People have been telling me for years that I ought to act sensibly. Now it seems that my first attempts to aren't meeting with your approval.' He sighed and turned serious. 'There's enough trouble here at the moment without my attempts to add to it, Karen.' He sounded a stranger again, and she knew he was resisting his natural desires. 'I don't want to complicate matters. You were right when you told me just after your arrival that it didn't help to mix business with pleasure. I don't want to involve you in anything that might harm your future career. You're not like an ordinary girl. You're a nurse, and you're following your vocation.'

'What has that got to do with it?' Karen demanded, and she realized with a start that she was now playing a reverse role. But pride didn't enter into it, she told herself. He had made her fall in love with him! She shuddered as she realized just how vulnerable she had become. Her main interest at the moment ought to have been the welfare of her patient, as it always had been, but she found that Mrs Murray was lying in second place in her mind. And there was no inner strength to enable her to fight this reversal! She knew that without searching her soul for the fact, and the knowledge seemed to weaken her still further.

'I'm sorry for what I've done to you, Karen,' he said slowly. 'I've been acting the fool for a very long time, and it's a pity I've come back to my sense of responsibility in the middle of trying to make you love me. But Duncan's accident has shocked me, and I can see where I've been going wrong all these years. I don't want to follow in my father's footsteps. He was a dreadful man, a bad husband and a fearsome father. He tried to instil hatred into us instead of love, and I rebelled against him. That should have finished me as far as being a Murray is concerned, but Mother is finding new strength again and we're going to beat this ugly inheritance.'

'I'm afraid I don't understand the half of it,' she protested. 'I want to do everything I can to help, Roy. You know that. But I'm so mixed up at the moment.'

'I'm sorry.' He pulled her gently back into his arms and kissed her. 'I haven't helped you any, have I? You've been doing a wonderful job with my mother. I wouldn't want to hurt you for anything in the world. I intended toying with your affections in the first place, especially when I saw how determined you were not to become involved. It was a kind of challenge, and I never could resist a challenge. But this has back-fired on me, Karen. I've begun to feel too much for you. I'm so very sorry, because I don't think anything could ever come of our getting together.'

She withdrew slowly from his arms, her face expressionless, her eyes not showing the hurt she was feeling. She nodded slowly.

'Perhaps I've needed this lesson,' she said. 'I have been forgetting my position here. I shouldn't have permitted myself the luxury of becoming involved. It's never happened before, and I prided myself upon my professionalism.'

'You don't have to blame yourself,' he said firmly. 'I'm the culprit.'

'No.' She shook her head slowly. 'I think I would have fallen for you no matter the situation.'

'Is that a fact?' His face slowly changed expression, and she saw a brightness touch his brown eyes. Then a wistful expression chased away the momentary hope and he shook his head. 'There's too much coming between us,' he said slowly. 'I wish there was a chance.'

Karen felt the wish to argue with him that nothing could prevent them finding happiness, but the expression in his eyes chilled her and she guessed there was more to the situation than she knew. Again she wondered about Duncan's accident, and it was in her to question him, but he continued talking, making her listen just with the quality of his low tones.

'You should see more of Doctor Sloan,' he said. 'I can tell that he has a high regard for you. You went out with him once, and you enjoyed yourself.'

'Only because it made a change,' she retorted. 'I knew that evening that

Doctor Sloan would never mean anything to me.'

He smiled slowly. 'It's a fact that a person can tell in a short time whether or not someone is going to be important. I had that feeling about you, Karen. I was almost as surprised as you when I kissed you that afternoon we met.'

She smiled at the memory, and he drew her closer into his embrace and kissed her.

'Don't play with my affections,' she said when he released her reluctantly.

'I wouldn't do that, although that is what I started out to do. You must give me time to think things out, Karen. We must see how Duncan comes back to us.'

'What do you think happened to him that afternoon?' she asked quietly, and he studied her face before replying.

'I wouldn't know. I must admit that I was surprised it happened.'

'How was it he had the dog with him?' She didn't take her eyes from his face, and she knew her suspicions were shining in her blue eyes. 'Blint belongs to you, doesn't he? Shouldn't he have gone with you to the cabin?'

'No.' He shook his head. 'Blint belongs to the Hall. I made a closer friend of him than Duncan ever did, but we took it in turns exercising the animal. I wouldn't take Blint to the cabin because his place is here.'

'I'm puzzled because I heard that Duncan's life had been threatened, Roy. Why should that be? How did he make such an enemy? I didn't think he looked the kind of man to harm anyone enough to warrant threats being made against his life.'

'There's a lot you don't know,' he replied thinly. 'It all had to do with that previous nurse, the one who nursed my father. I was attracted to her, but she wasn't so important to me. She seemed to think she was, and she was out to better herself. When she realized that I had no intention of falling in love with her she turned her attentions to

Duncan, and he fell for her. Duncan never had anything to do with women, and I could see what kind of a girl this was, trying to get into the Hall as mistress no matter what it took. So I began to play up to her with the intention of saving Duncan from her. It all seems so melodramatic now, but at the time I could think of no other way. Duncan didn't like it, of course, and the situation was complicated by the fact that he felt guilty because I was first interested in the girl. He thought he was taking her away from me and I played this up for all I was worth in order to make a break.' He shook his head slowly, and there was bitterness in his voice. 'It eventually came out the way I wanted, but there was a dreadful scene at the end, and the girl realized that I had compromised her in Duncan's eyes and ruined all her chances. The strange thing was, she didn't blame me for this, but she intended that Duncan should pay for her failure to get into the Hall as mistress. Duncan's life was threatened, and the police were informed. They checked up on the girl's brother, and seemed satisfied that what had happened was not serious. But now this accident to Duncan may be more serious than we think, and I have informed the police of my suspicions.'

Karen felt relief seep into her mind at his words. She had felt the weight of her suspicions directed at him, and knew the pain of half believing them, but what he had said made her realize that he cared for Duncan far more than he showed, and he couldn't possibly have been responsible for what happened to his brother. She began to think that it had been an unfortunate accident after all.

'You seem to be losing your worries,' he remarked, watching her intently. 'I'm sorry you've had so much to occupy your mind, and I'll do what I can in future to help you along. I know how much you're helping my mother, and for that alone I can't thank you enough.'

'You owe me no thanks,' Karen said gently. Her eyes were shining and there was a faint bloom to her cheeks that heightened her expression. 'I'm only doing my job, Roy.'

'It's more than a job for you,' he retorted. 'How shall I ever be able to thank you for what you're doing?'

'I'm worried about what might happen if your mother finds out about Duncan before she's in a position to withstand such a shock. Do you think we'll be able to keep it from her?'

'I don't see why not. Duncan has gone off before on business, and this is the time of year when he takes a short holiday.'

'Perhaps, but he sees his mother before he goes, doesn't he?' she demanded.

'Usually, but we can put her off. When do you expect to get her out of bed?'

'Next week. Doctor Sloan is keen for her to show that she wants to get up before we talk to her about attempting it. I'm beginning to pave the way with my conversations, but she might begin looking for Duncan once she starts getting around, and he won't be out of hospital for quite some time.'

'He's not even out of the wood yet,' Roy agreed. 'I wonder what he was doing in that part of the moors! He knows enough about this area to take the elementary precautions. But from what I've deduced, he acted like a complete idiot.'

'Did he go there to meet someone?' she demanded, and he stared at her speculatively.

'That's something I've been asking myself,' he replied slowly. 'I've been looking through his desk, hoping to find a letter, or something, but obviously he wouldn't leave anything lying around.'

Karen nodded, and felt that the whole situation was clouded by mystery. When she thought that the police might uncover something, and considered the effect any disclosures might have upon Mrs Murray, she felt alarmed, and determined to do whatever she could to guard against any shocks which might arise. But only a part of her mind was concentrating upon her duties, and she knew life would never be the same again for her. Meeting Roy Murray had laid the groundwork for eternal changes.

He was still very close to her, and Karen could feel the tug of his presence. She wanted to get back into his embrace, and wondered that her habitual reserve should crumble so quickly and completely before him. She could hardly recognize herself now, and this was only the beginning! In another week or two she would be completely under Roy's spell.

He must have read something of her thoughts because he smiled and pulled her into his arms.

'I don't care what is right or wrong here,' he said firmly, and again there was hope shining in his dark eyes. 'All I know is that I need you, Karen, and you're keen to need me.' He smiled as he studied her lovely face. 'You're the most beautiful girl I've ever met, and I don't have to wonder why it was that I never fell in love before. I've been waiting for you to come along. You're the right girl all right!'

'What makes you so sure?' She was trembling with excitement, and he gathered her into his arms. Nothing else seemed to matter in that moment, and she closed her eyes as she felt as if she were being borne away on a magic carpet of ecstasy.

A knock at the door interrupted them and startled Karen, and she drew guiltily away from him as he smiled and called out an invitation to enter. Deidre came into the room, pausing on the threshold to glance at them, and there was a tiny smile on the girl's attractive face. Karen realized that the maid guessed at their secret, and she felt a little warmth seep into her breast as she realized that the girl approved.

'Doctor Sloan is here,' the girl announced. 'He would like to see Nurse Gregory.'

'Show him into the front lounge,

Deidre,' Roy said, 'and tell him Nurse Gregory will be down in a moment.'

'Yes.' The girl smiled and departed, and Karen stood watching Roy as if her life depended upon it. He waited for the door to close, then came to her side again.

'He's interested in you, Karen,' he said slowly. 'Are you sure you couldn't find something with Sloan? He's a very nice man, and one who would adore a girl like you.'

'No.' She shook her head emphatically. 'Don't try to find me someone, Roy. I'm not interested in anyone.' She paused, then added: 'except you.' A smile flickered across his face and was gone, and then he nodded slowly.

'That's the answer I was hoping you'd give, but I don't see a clear avenue for us, Karen. I want to spare you trouble, but it seems there's nothing but that lying ahead of me!'

'Why should you say that?' she demanded. 'What trouble could there possibly be?'

'It's all tied up with my father's will. I won't go into the details, but if Duncan ever married he would lose his position here and forfeit everything to which he is at present entitled.'

'How could your father make such a will?' she demanded.

'That's a question I can never answer for myself,' he said shortly. 'I am not similarly affected, because my father had cut me off before he died. Perhaps that's one of the reasons why I'm half afraid to take a chance with a woman. I might turn out to be like my father, or perhaps my children might.'

She watched him intently, and saw real worry in his face. A pang of sympathy touched her. No-one should have such dark thoughts in mind, she thought, and wished there was something she could do to reassure him.

'But I'm almost willing to take every chance just to have the pleasure of knowing you, Karen,' he said. She could not hold herself from him as he placed his hands upon her shoulders, and he began to draw her into the circle of his arms once more. Then she remembered Phelan Sloan was waiting for her, and she drew back with a little start of regret.

'I'd better go see Doctor Sloan,' she said apologetically. 'Will you be in here when I come back?'

'No.' He shook his head. 'I'm going out shortly. But I'll be back later, and perhaps we can continue this. I've got so much on my mind at the moment, but I can see that I'll have to do something about you.'

She stared into his face for a moment, wondering what was passing through his mind, and she could not help telling herself that she was in love with him. He was becoming very important, and nothing she could do would alter the fact. He pressed her hands and then let her go, and walked to the door with her, his expression sad but hopeful. She suppressed a sigh as she left him, and when she reached the doorway of the front lounge she paused and looked back at him. He was ascending the stairs, and she let her expression soften as she watched him. What had aroused her passions? How had he managed to get through her guard? What was there about him that made him so different? She shook her head, feeling helpless and subdued, and her mind was filled with conjecture as she entered the room where Phelan Sloan was waiting.

He came towards the door to meet her, his face showing concern, and she wondered what had happened to bring him. A pang of worry touched her as she imagined that Duncan's condition had deteriorated and that Sloan had come to warn them.

'Hello, Karen,' he greeted, smiling thinly. 'I had to come and see you. I hope I haven't disturbed you from anything more important.'

'Is it about Duncan?' she demanded.

'No. I've asked the hospital to keep me informed of his condition, and the latest report is that nothing has changed.'

'I hope he'll soon start showing signs of recovering consciousness,' Karen said, moving to a seat. The big room was warm, for there was a log burning in the massive grate, and there was no need for the small, ornate chandelier that was alight just above Phelan's head. The leaping flames filled the room with bright animation, and there was a sense of cosiness that touched Karen's heart.

'There's no telling in a case like this,' he responded, coming to join her, and he held her gaze with his steady blue eyes. 'But in the circumstances there is cause for worry. I'd like to know exactly what happened to him that afternoon, and I know the police are waiting for the chance to question him.'

'What do you think happened?' she questioned.

He shrugged and shook his head. 'It wouldn't help to guess, but I would say that the sooner the situation is cleared up the better.'

'I agree with you. But what was it you

wanted to see me about, Phelan?'

He smiled, and looked away for a moment to stare into the fire. They were sitting within the large circle of its radiance, and Karen could feel her cheeks getting warm from the glow. When he looked back at her his smile was gone and his expresion was most serious.

'We've changed from doctor and nurse into something more friendly, more human,' he said slowly. 'But something has happened to you since our first evening out together, Karen. Perhaps I was being foolish in hoping that friendship might blossom between us, then ripen into something more promising, but that hasn't come about, and now I'm finding that you're beginning to interfere with my work. I've got you on my mind and I can't seem to do anything about it. All I can do is ask you out again, and hope that something will come of it.'

When he paused and regarded her, Karen felt something shrivel in her heart. She stared into his handsome face, and felt something of the tension that filled him. There was hope shining in his pale eyes, and the brightness there wasn't wholly to do with the glow of the fire. She felt a pang touch her, and unhappiness came to her when she realized that she had to dash his hopes. Roy Murray had her in his power too completely for her to ever consider breaking away, and it was obvious to her that she didn't want to change that particular situation. She made no reply to Sloan's question while she wondered how best to answer him without hurting him, and he seemed to read her silence right, for he drew a sharp breath and leaned back in his chair.

'I think you'd better forget that question, Karen,' he said softly. 'I can tell by your expression that your reply wouldn't be favourable, and I think I know why. I hope from the bottom of my heart that you're not making a wrong decision, because I'd hate to see you get hurt. It's Roy Murray, isn't it?'

He smiled grimly and got to his feet to pace the carpet in front of the fire. 'You don't have to answer that,' he told her shortly. 'I have no right to pry into your affairs. But I do feel responsible for you, having brought you here in the first place, and I can't help feeling that there is more to this business of Duncan than is apparent. However time will tell, and all we can do is hope for the best.'

Karen found herself thinking along the same lines, and her heart seemed to swell as she prayed that Roy had not been implicated in his brother's accident. But the waiting to find out was becoming more difficult by the hour, and she had to take a grip upon her imagination in order to prevent it running riot.

'I'm sorry, Phelan,' she said quietly. 'If our going out together on that evening has given you the impression that we might become more than friends then it's my fault. I wouldn't want to hurt you in any way. But as you so rightly guess, there isn't a chance that we could come to mean more to one another. I'd rather not say more about where my true feelings lie. I don't think I really know that myself.'

'And I have no right to ask,' he said quickly. 'Let's forget that I came here this evening, Karen, and perhaps we can remain upon our usual level of friendship. I'd better be going now, anyway. I have a special call to make, and was on my way when I dropped by.' He came to her and patted her shoulder. 'I hope everything works out all right for you.'

She walked with him to the door, and already her mind was in pursuit of Roy. She couldn't stop herself thinking of him! Sloan departed and she went back to the front lounge, but there was no peace of mind for her, and the more she considered what Sloan had said the worse her uneasiness seemed. She was in love for the first time in her life, and the way ahead seemed blocked by uncertainty and trouble. It wouldn't help to worry about it, but she was only human, and the waiting period that seemed to lie between her and the fulfilment or failure of her dreams was like an insurmountable barrier filling her whole horizon . . .

10

In the following two days Karen found the time dragging as it had never done before. She saw little of Roy, and the news from the hospital was always the same; no change in Duncan's condition. Mrs Murray asked innumerable questions about Duncan, until she was satisfied that business was keeping her eldest son away from Glen Hall. Karen was apprehensive about the woman's condition. If anything in the nature of a shock came along then all the good work that had been done for Mrs Murray would be undone in a flash.

Roy seemed to alternate between great optimism and grey despair on the few occasions when Karen saw him. She began to feel that he was worried about his brother's recovery, because Duncan might have something to say that would incriminate Roy. She tried to subdue her suspicions, but was never really successful, and each passing day added its own pile of worry to her slim shoulders, the accumulative total weighing very heavily upon her.

When Mrs Murray began to get out of bed, for an hour at first, then for progressively longer periods, Karen was hard put to contain the woman's curiosity. It was now three weeks since Duncan met with his accident, and it was becoming increasingly obvious that soon his mother would have to be told the truth. Karen raised the question with Phelan Sloan when he called one afternoon, and the doctor hesitated before answering.

'I wouldn't like to take the chance yet,' he said finally. 'I have no way of knowing what the news will do to her.'

'But she is becoming more pressing with her questions about Duncan,' Karen pointed out. 'It's all very well for me to keep telling her that he's away on a holiday that's combined with business, but she wants to know why he doesn't write or phone. I think she is strong enough to know something of the truth.'

'You won't be able to tell her part of it,' he retorted. 'It will be all or nothing. She'll get at the rest with questions if you only tell her part of it. She'll know that Duncan must be seriously ill if he's been in hospital for three weeks with a head injury.'

'Isn't he ever going to regain consciousness?' Karen demanded despairingly. 'I don't think I can stand the suspense much longer.'

'You have my sympathies.' He stared into her face for a moment, then tightened his grip upon his medical bag. 'Come on, let's go and acquaint Mrs Murray with the news of Duncan's accident. We'll have to hope for the best, that's all, but it will relieve you of some of the tension if she knows the worst about her son.'

'Perhaps I'd better tell her,' Karen suggested. 'She trusts me implicitly now.'

'She couldn't fail to do so,' he remarked. 'I could find you several nursing jobs around here, Karen, if you're interested after you've finished with Mrs Murray.'

'I'd rather not think about the future just yet,' she replied with a little smile touching her lips. Her blue eyes were gentle, but her face showed signs of her inner worry.

'I'll wait here until you've told her about Duncan,' Sloan said. 'I'd better be on hand in case the shock is too much for her.'

Karen nodded. They had slowly ascended the stairs to the sick room, and she entered alone, to find her patient sitting propped up in her bed, her eyes fixed in an unwavering stare on the scenery outside her window.

'Mrs Murray, I want to talk to you,' Karen said immediately, knowing that any hesitation would rob her of her determination. She almost lost her nerve when the woman turned her large brown eyes towards her. There was a world of painful experience glimmering in their dark depths. A lifetime of suffering stoically showed in the lines of countenance, and Karen didn't want to be the one to add more to an already over-weighed soul.

'Is it about Duncan?' Mrs Murray demanded.

Karen almost lost her nerve in that moment, and she wondered just how much this woman could define by intuition.

'It is about Duncan,' she said slowly.

'I've guessed for some time that there was more to his absence than you've told me.' The directness of the woman's gaze held Karen's eyes against her will, and her lips moved soundlessly as she tried to go on.

'Anything that has been suppressed was done so because of your condition,' Karen said. 'But you don't have to worry about Duncan. He did have an accident, as you so rightly guessed so many times. He's in hospital now, but his condition is satisfactory.'

'What happened to him?' There were other questions in the woman's mind, and they showed as a cloud in her dark eyes.

'He was out walking on the moors, and a rock fell from a ridge and struck him on the head.' Karen was aware as she spoke that the story didn't ring true, and she didn't miss the expression which came to life in the woman's eyes.

'Are you sure that's what happened?' she demanded sharply.

'That's it exactly! I wouldn't lie to you, Mrs Murray.'

'I don't think you would. I've never met a more likeable girl, Nurse. You've certainly proved your worth to me. But you've become involved with the situation here, haven't you?'

'I don't think so!' Karen shook her head, knowing her words to be false. 'I've always made a point of remaining aloof from everything connected with my patient. It's the first golden rule.'

'I know!' A faint smile touched Mrs Murray's lips. 'But this involvement of yours is much against your will, and I know you are not responsible. You see, Roy has spoken to me about you.'

'Has he?' Karen frowned. 'I have no

idea what he might have said.'

'Let's talk about Duncan, shall we?' Mrs Murray changed the subject adroitly. 'Even if he is in hospital with a head injury, why hasn't he spoken to me over the telephone? That would have reassured me. I've seen you growing more worried each day. I would like to have the full facts. I can take it, you know. I'm a tough old woman despite my looks.'

'He's never regained consciousness since the accident,' Karen said slowly.

Mrs Murray was silent for a moment, her face stern as her fears struggled to gain control of her mind, but she fought back and resisted.

'He should be all right soon,' Karen said hopefully. 'I'm sure there's nothing to worry about, Mrs Murray.'

'Where was Roy when this accident happened?' the older woman demanded, and Karen felt her heart flutter at the question.

'Roy was on his way to the cabin,' she said. 'That's a strange question, Mrs Murray.'

'It may seem so to you, but I have my reasons for asking.'

'You think Roy might be responsible for Duncan's accident?' Karen could not help but ask the question. The suspicions which had been riding her since the day of the accident seemed to gather in her mind and try to burst through her defences.

'I wouldn't say that!' Mrs Murray's voice was sharp, and Karen stared at her for a moment, wondering what was passing through the woman's mind. 'I don't know what stories you've heard about my sons, but I assure you that Roy wouldn't hurt his brother. I am not sure about Duncan's actions under certain circumstances, but Roy is fairly open-minded, and it is quite simple to read him.'

'But you questioned his whereabouts when the accident happened,' Karen persisted. 'It sounded very suspicious to me.'

'Perhaps my thoughts were turning in a different direction.' Mrs Murray smiled. 'Duncan rarely goes out on to the moors. I couldn't help wondering if Duncan had followed Roy out there.'

'To harm him?' Karen could not keep the surprise out of her tones.

'That is possible.' Mrs Murray inclined her head, and her face was set in serious lines. 'There was a lot of trouble between my two sons when my husband's nurse was here. No doubt you've heard about that. It was mainly Duncan's fault. I'm not trying to whiten Roy, but he acted the more sensibly, and if Duncan hadn't been so selfish he would have realized that.' The woman shrugged. 'If it had been Roy found injured out there I would have been upset by the implications that would have arisen in my mind. But I'm sure that Duncan's injuries were sustained entirely accidentally.'

'I hope you're right,' Karen said fervently.

'I'm sure I am.' Mrs Murray smiled. 'Is it Doctor Sloan outside? I heard you talking to someone before you came in.'

'Yes, he was waiting in case the news of Duncan upset you.' Karen smiled her relief.

'If it had been Roy perhaps I would have needed the doctor's help,' the woman replied. 'Ask him to come in now, will you?'

Karen did so with alacrity. She left the doctor talking with her patient and went down to the kitchen, hoping that Roy was there, and her heart seemed to miss a beat when she saw him seated at the table. He smiled at her and got to his feet, and he seemed as if a great weight had lifted from his shoulders. For a moment she thought she had let her heart blind her eyes, but he came towards her, lifting a hand to her shoulders.

'Where have you been hiding yourself today?' he demanded.

'I haven't been hiding myself at all,' she countered, glancing past him at the housekeeper, who was actually smiling. The woman nodded her head slowly, as if to say that she agreed with Roy's light-heartedness. Karen was surprised, and let the emotion show in her face.

'What does the doctor have to say about my mother now?' Roy demanded.

'All his reports are showing her great progress. She'll soon be coming down the stairs,' Karen told him.

'Will she stand the shock of knowing exactly what happened to Duncan?'

'I told her a few minutes ago, and she took it very well.' Karen frowned as she studied his intent face.

'I said exactly what happened to Duncan,' he retorted.

'What exactly did happen?' Karen had the feeling that there were new developments in the situation, and her pulses leaped as she began to hope that Roy himself could prove that he had nothing at all to do with the accident. Her own mind was not completely clear of doubt.

'I had a call from the local police a short time ago,' Roy said, and he could not keep a faint trace of his relief from his tones. 'They've found someone who was on the moors that afternoon Duncan had his accident. They want me to go along to the police station tomorrow morning so this man can look me over. He says he saw Duncan on the afternoon in question, and also another man whom he would know again.'

'Then the police suspect you!' Karen said heavily, and there was a sudden pang of despair threading its way through her mind.

'No.' His face showed a number of emotions, most of them happy, but there was a tinge of worry in his dark eyes. 'It's a matter of elimination, that's all.'

'That's what they call it, but the fact remains,' she said carefully.

'You don't think I'd do a thing like that, do you?' he asked in challenging tones.

Karen was aware that Amena Lachlan stood staring at her from across the kitchen, and the woman's face was unfriendly again. She suppressed a sigh as she answered.

'Roy, it's not for me to think

anything. I don't want to think about it. It wouldn't be fair to either of us if I had to try and make up my mind to anything, one way or another.'

'I'm sorry.' He looked troubled. 'Of course I can't ask you to decide. I know I'm not guilty of anything, but it has to be proved to everyone else. I ought to be grateful for the chance to prove it.' He nodded slowly. 'You'll see, Karen. I shall come out of this with a clean bill of health.'

'I'm glad you're so confident.' Karen smiled, but she wasn't feeling happy about his news. If the police wanted him in an identification parade then they must suspect him. She shook her head as she tried to divorce herself from the situation. It was none of her business! She told herself so in fierce undertones, but she knew that her love for Roy involved her considerably, and facing the fact filled her with despair. But she couldn't blame him. She had only herself to blame for falling in love with him, for permitting her golden rule to be broken. But love was a gift from the gods, and was not bestowed lightly. It came in the most unexpected ways, and when it struck there was little a girl could do about it.

'Why shouldn't I be confident?' He was smiling now.

'I don't know. I have so many strange feelings.' Karen spoke slowly, aware that Amena Lachlan was smiling again. 'There has been so much unexplained that I don't have enough of the pieces to form a complete picture.'

'I can understand that.' He came to her side. 'It's a complex situation, and I don't thank my father's memory for the trouble he willed to us. But that is slowly being sorted out to everyone's satisfaction, perhaps with the exception of Duncan, and I don't think we need to worry about it any more. When we know that Duncan is out of the wood we'll be able to take a deep breath and carry on where we all left off.'

She nodded, aware that she wanted to do just that. He looked into her face, searching for some sign that she agreed, and he must have liked the expression in her eyes because he smiled.

'Are you busy right now?' he demanded.

'No. I've half an hour.'

'Then let's go out into the garden and have a few moments on our own.'

'You can't go out there,' Amena said quickly. 'It's been raining all morning.'

'Since when have I worried about the weather?' he demanded. 'I don't know so much about Karen, but I'm willing to wager that she is the same type of girl.'

'I'll get my coat,' she said, and left the kitchen, feeling far happier than she had been for some time.

They walked across the wet lawns. The sun was shining now, but the obvious signs of autumn were all about them. The trees were shedding their leaves, the flowerbeds were looking bare and desolate, and Karen could feel something of the wistfulness of the time of year. It filled her with an unreasoning uneasiness that was hard to shake off, but she fought against her intuitive feelings that the worst of the trouble was yet to come. Looking at Roy's strong and handsome face, she told herself that trouble would have no chance against him. He would overcome all obstacles, and claim her in the name of love.

'My mother is making wonderful progress now,' he remarked as they passed out of sight of the house. 'All thanks are due to you, Karen. Shortly mother won't need a nurse at all. I shall keep you on here for as long as possible, but there will come a time when you've got to go. What will you do?'

She studied his face for a moment, still largely unaware of what his inner thoughts were like. He had professed love for her! He had denied himself once, when he thought that the dictates of the estate would be against him looking upon her in a favourable light. Did he still believe that he was in love with her? She could not tell by his expression, and she shrugged a little hopelessly as she tried to find an adequate answer.

'I shall have to take another nursing job somewhere,' she said slowly.

'I know! I was speaking with Sloan yesterday. He seems to think that he could find you enough nursing work around here to keep you busy for the rest of your career. Would you like to stay around here, or won't you be able to get away from us quickly enough?'

'I think I'd like to stay for as long as possible.' She spoke with caution in her tones, trying to disguise her eagerness. She wouldn't give any sign of what she was feeling. If he had enough interest then he would make it obvious, and when she saw those signs she would know what to do.

'Then speak to Sloan about it as soon as possible,' he said earnestly. 'It will relieve me of a lot of worry if I can know that you won't be leaving us for good. I'd have to come and find you,

Karen, if you went far away.'

'Would you?' she spoke breathlessly, her pulses racing again, her heart seeming to labour under the sudden load of emotion which filtered through her.

'Yes!' He spoke slowly, holding her gaze, and she could feel the strength going from her. She felt vulnerable and open to his powers, and he knew, because his eyes proclaimed that he had knowledge of her love for him, and that knowledge placed him in an omniscient position. She could not tell what was passing through his mind, and it bothered her. She was at his mercy, and could only hope that he would not treat her harshly. She knew so little about him, and there wouldn't be much time in which to learn all that she needed to know. But her instincts wouldn't play her wrong and she knew she had to trust them for all they were worth.

He glanced around, then took her into his arms. She closed her eyes as all those new and wonderful emotions tore through her. This was all that mattered. She was dimly aware of thinking so. She clung to him with all her strength, trying to inform him by her own powers that she was in love with him and wanted him. When he kissed her she quivered as if she had been struck, and the pressure of his mouth against hers was sufficient to warn her that she would never be able to free herself from his power. She was his slave and, if he discovered that, she would be completely in his hands. But she hoped and prayed that he would treat her gently. If he didn't mean what he was implying then she would suffer when the time for parting and disillusionment came. She had to trust him, and it came home to her then in no uncertain manner that the greater part of love consisted of trust. Having decided that, she felt easier in her mind and some of the worries fell away.

She would trust him until he gave her cause to doubt the wisdom of that decision. If he loved her as he said he did then he would never give her cause for regret, and that was all she would ask for.

11

For the first time in her life Karen found herself counting the hours and the days. Each day now seemed like a lifetime, and she was filled with anticipation that was agony to bear. She didn't know what to expect in the way of developments, but she could not keep her fears from dominating her mind. She knew she ought to have confidence in Roy, but the fact that Duncan lay gravely ill in hospital and the police were making investigations seemed to point to the conclusion that Duncan's injuries had not been caused by an accident, and that was where the ominous note crept into Karen's life.

But Mrs Murray began to make immeasurable progress. Each new day found her that much better, and soon she was getting up for several hours daily. The woman's face began to show her progress, and Karen realized with a pang of regret that very soon her services would no longer be required. She began to find herself in the unenviable position of wishing time would stand still for her and at the same time hoping that the days would pass more quickly in order that the mystery surrounding Duncan's accident might be cleared up.

Roy made it clear that he was beginning to accept the fact that Karen was important to him. She noticed the slight changes in his manner, the imperceptible warming to her that came to him. He found the time and the opportunity each day to spend precious minutes in her company, and Karen knew she was now hopelessly in love with him. He showed tenderness and understanding in his treatment of her, and seemed to know that she was suspicious of Duncan's accident. He accepted her cautiousness, and Karen felt mean as she tried to subdue her natural instincts and let love rule her heart.

Mrs Murray finally came down from

her room, and Karen was anxious that morning as she helped the woman negotiate the stairs. She accompanied her patient around the house, and there was a tense moment when they entered the kitchen. In all the time that she had been at Glen Hall, Karen had not seen Mrs Murray face to face with Amena Lachlan, and now she watched both women closely as they met.

Amena almost curtsied, and Karen was surprised. She hadn't thought the housekeeper had so much respect in her. Mrs. Murray was gentle and gracious. She was a little unsteady on her feet, and Karen remained at her side, holding her arm to support her. They sat down at the table and Mrs Murray asked for coffee. Amena scurried around the kitchen to prepare it. Deidre came into the kitchen, and was loud in her pleasure at seeing her mistress.

'You've been keeping the rooms spotless,' Mrs Murray said, and Deidre fairly bloomed with pleasure.

'I'm so happy that you're almost well again, Mrs Murray,' the maid retorted. 'The Hall hasn't been the same place with you ill in that room. I'm sure it was a great idea of Doctor Sloan's to have a nurse in.' She smiled at Karen, who nodded slowly.

'I'm relieved that I've made such a good recovery,' Mrs Murray said.

'But don't make the mistake of thinking you're completely well,' Karen warned. 'If you try to do too much you'll put yourself back into that bed in no time.'

'I know, and I'm not going to take any chances. You won't think of leaving yet, will you?'

'Well my work here is almost at an end, I'm glad to say,' Karen told her.

'You've not been unhappy here?' There was concern in Mrs Murray's tones.

'No. I'm glad because you're almost well. I'm always happy when it's time for me to leave a case, not because I have any personal feelings about the position, but because it means a successful conclusion and a return to health by my patient.'

'Well you're not to consider leaving now, just because I'm almost back to normal. I want you to stay for at least another month, Karen.'

Karen did not answer, but her heart seemed to leap with sudden excitement. She took advantage of Amena's coffee to change the subject.

'Doctor Sloan told me last evening that Duncan is expected to regain consciousness soon. He's beginning to show signs of coming to.'

'I'm sure he'll be all right,' Mrs Murray said. 'Roy tells me that the estate is being run adequately. My husband would never let Roy take part in the administration. But now he's proved himself, and he wants to continue doing something around the place. There are going to be a lot of changes here when Duncan does return.' She looked at Amena as she spoke, and the housekeeper nodded slowly.

Karen wondered at the situation which had reigned in the Hall before Mrs Murray's illness, and she could not help thinking that the woman had not been the complete mistress. But there was a streak of determination in the woman's tones, and Karen knew now why she had been asked to stay at least another month. Mrs Murray wanted an ally, and there could be no-one to be better trusted than her own private nurse.

But there were no protests from Amena Lachlan, and Karen could not help wondering how this situation would finally settle itself. She knew Roy's father had been responsible for much of the friction, but all that should have died with the man's death.

Mrs Murray went back to bed early in the afternoon to rest, but she was determined to get up again later, and Karen hoped she was not about to experience difficulties now the worst part of Mrs Murray's illness was over.

Doctor Sloan arrived earlier than

usual that afternoon, and Karen could tell by his expression that he had momentous news.

'Is Mrs Murray awake?' he demanded.

'I expect she's asleep now, Phelan. She went up to rest only a few minutes ago.'

'I was at the hospital half an hour ago,' he told her. 'Duncan recovered consciousness for a few minutes this morning, and they expect him to be awake this evening. Of course his injuries are healing well. There are no complications with that skull fracture. When he does recover full consciousness he'll be almost well enough to leave hospital.'

'It's been a long time since his accident,' Karen said, and she was aware of a gathering fear inside her.

'He asked to speak to you,' Sloan said, his blue eyes showing speculation.

'Me?' she echoed in surprise.

'And he doesn't want to see Roy under any circumstances.' Sloan kept his voice steady.

'I would like to know exactly what

does trouble this family.' Karen was trying to keep her curiosity in check. Without all the facts she was unable to get a clear picture. She was involved now, and there was no going back. Whatever happened in this family circle would affect her.

'I wouldn't know enough to be able to tell you anything,' he said, 'and probably the stories that I've heard aren't all true. I hope you know what you're doing here, Karen.' There was genuine concern in his tones, and she nodded slowly.

'I'd better ring the hospital and get them to let me know when Duncan recovers consciousness again. I'll stand by to go and see him.' Karen was already wondering why he wanted to see her and why he had been so adamant about not seeing his brother. It seemed ominous to her, and she didn't like the worries that started filling her mind. It was then she recalled that Roy hadn't told her what had happened at the identification parade he'd attended a few days before, and she resolved to ask him.

'I won't disturb Mrs Murray now, if she is resting,' Sloan said. 'I'll be on my way, Karen.' He paused and studied her face, and she had the feeling that there was a lot more he wished to say to her. But he shook his head slowly and turned to leave. She stood at the door watching him until his car had gone from sight. Then she went thoughtfully in search of Roy, and found him in the library, at the desk.

'What did the doctor want?' Roy asked, getting up from the desk, and Karen watched his face closely as she told him about Duncan's recovery. 'That's great news!' His manner warmed instantly. Then she told him that Duncan had no wish to see him. His eyes narrowed, but the relief did not leave his face. 'So long as he's getting better!' he said. 'I don't care about our personal differences.'

'Do you think he believes you struck him down, Roy?' she demanded.

'You still don't trust me!' The

knowledge seemed to hurt him, and she was sorry she had spoken.

'It isn't that, Roy,' she said slowly. 'There's so much that cannot be explained. But Duncan himself should be able to throw some light upon this mystery when he fully regains consciousness. What do the police think about all this?'

'They haven't told me.' His tones suggested that he would be the last one to know. 'But if you're still concerned about my future then you'd better know that the witness they found couldn't identify me as the stranger he saw that afternoon he spotted Duncan on the moors.'

'Well that's a relief!' Karen expelled her pent up breath in a long sigh. 'Why didn't you tell me before, Roy?'

'Because I knew it wouldn't help you to make up your mind one way or another.' He smiled thinly. 'You're going to stay on for at least another month, aren't you?'

'Your mother asked me to.' Karen

smiled at his adroit change of subject. 'Was it her wish or have you been whispering in her ear?'

'And if I admit that it was partly my idea?' He watched her closely, his dark eyes filled with an undefinable emotion.

'I'll stay,' she told him.

'Good. Mother will need watching, you know. She's always been prone to shrugging off any illness and getting back into harness before time. But this time she's got to be careful. We almost lost her, and I don't want anything happening to her for a long time yet.'

'I agree with you. But she is a good patient, and I'm sure she will have the sense to realize that she might kill herself by being too eager to forget this illness.'

'I'm more concerned about you!' He came towards her eagerly, holding out his arms for her to enter his embrace, but she denied herself the pleasure, holding up her hands to press the palms against his broad chest.

'Roy, please don't.' She couldn't even

guess why she went against her instincts. 'I'm under your spell as it is, and you are complicating matters. Let us wait until we know what Duncan has to say about his accident.'

His face fell, and he moistened his lips, his eyes suddenly blank and expressionless. 'You're not sure about me,' he accused gently. 'You're afraid that Duncan will say I attacked him that afternoon, and if he does you'll fly from here as fast as you can pack. Is that the measure of your love for me, Karen?'

'No!' She spoke desperately. 'That isn't what I mean, Roy. How can I explain what's in my mind? Everything seems so very complicated. I think it is just good sense to wait, don't you?'

'Perhaps you're right. All I hope is that you do love me.'

'How will Duncan accept the news, if we ever get around to telling him?' She watched his face intently, and saw worry come to his brown eyes.

'He'll have to get used to the idea,' he

said heavily. 'I don't think we have to worry about Duncan, Karen.' He took her into his arms and kissed her gently on the lips. Before she could push him away he released her, and she stood immobile, watching him, and her mind was beset by many strange and conflicting emotions.

It was the next day before Duncan regained consciousness again, and Roy drove Karen to the hospital. She felt apprehensive as she left him in the car, and she could tell by his expression that he was hurt by Duncan's refusal to see him. She was taken along to Duncan's room, and was surprised to see him sitting up in bed. There was a small square of bandage covering the area of his head which had been injured, and apart from a slight pallor in his cheeks he looked very much normal.

'Hello, Duncan,' she greeted him, and the attendant nurse departed.

'It was good of you to come,' he said in low tones.

'You asked to see me.' She was

impatient to learn what was on his mind. After weeks of speculation about Roy's involvement, she could hardly wait out the last moments to know what exactly had happened that afternoon on the moors.

'Yes.' He nodded slowly, his dark eyes fixed in a stare upon her face. 'I shall be coming home very soon now. I want to know that the situation there will be normal.'

'But that afternoon when you were injured!'

'I'm keeping the details to myself.' He smiled thinly, and she chilled at the sight of the triumph in his eyes. For a moment she wondered if his sanity had been affected by the injuries he had sustained. 'I don't have to ask you what has been happening at the Hall while I've been lying here. Roy wouldn't miss an opportunity like that. I suppose he's taken over my work on the estate?'

'Of course!' Karen inclined her blonde head. 'Someone had to take over, and Roy faced up to his duty.'

'And in his spare time he impressed you with his charm.'

Karen made no reply to that, and after a pause she said: 'Why did you ask me to come and see you, Duncan?'

'There is a reason!' His eyes brightened for a moment. 'I know you're dedicated to your work, and the health of your patient comes before all else. Isn't that so?'

'That's right.'

'That what I thought. I judged you correctly. You would do anything to see that my mother makes a complete recovery, wouldn't you?'

'Of course!'

'Well she will have a relapse if you stay on after your work with her has finished.'

'I don't understand.' Karen could feel a coldness seeping into her breast. She could tell by his eyes that he was deadly serious, and if he had any advantage in this situation then he would play it to the fullest extent.

'Of course you don't! I tried to warn

you off when I first realized that Roy was attracting you. I won't go into the details of what happened when the other nurse was at the Hall, but I was lucky there. I managed to show her up for what she was worth. She tried to ensnare Roy, and when I realized it I set myself to lure her away from him. I succeeded, because she was only interested in becoming the mistress of Glen Hall. Roy discovered, much to his mental confusion, that she wasn't worth considering, and shortly afterwards she left us.'

'You seem to have a different version of that story,' Karen said stiffly. 'But that doesn't concern me.'

'No!' He spoke harshly. 'But it concerns me a great deal. I will tell you this much. It concerns Roy a lot more. I've told the police about the afternoon I had my accident. I said that I can't remember what happened. I went out for a walk on the moors, and there's a blank from that time until I regained consciousness here in this bed. But that isn't the truth, Nurse. I saw the man who struck me down. It was my brother Roy!'

'No!' Karen ejaculated the word through stiff lips. She shook her head. 'I know Roy well enough now to judge him correctly. He's not capable of doing something like that.'

'You may think what you like!' He smiled thinly, and his eyes had no warmth. 'All I have to do is tell the police that I've suddenly regained my memory and that Roy struck me down. He won't be able to prove that he didn't do it, and no-one will suspect that I have a motive for wanting Roy to take the blame.'

'You wouldn't ruin his life like that!'

'I would, and I will!' He was smiling broadly now. 'I know Roy doesn't have an alibi for that afternoon. He told me the morning before that he was going to the cabin for a few days.'

'Then you know that he didn't have anything to do with your accident! He didn't strike you!'

'I can't remember.' His eyes showed triumph, and Karen could not help wondering what was in the back of his mind.

'You're lying,' she retorted. 'I'll believe nothing against your brother.'

'It doesn't matter what you think,' he retorted. 'But I'll tell you what I want. You're to leave the Hall as soon as possible and not communicate with Roy in any way.'

'And if I refuse?' Karen could not keep the dullness out of her tones.

'I shall suddenly regain my memory and accuse Roy of attempting to murder me. He has a motive, you know, and everyone in this locality knows of it. My father cut him out of the will completely, and Roy never bothered to fight it. He inherits only upon my death. That's motive enough for the police, and I've left a sealed letter with the family solicitor to point the guilt in the right direction.'

'But this was an accident that happened to you?' Karen questioned.

'It is important for me to know.'

'I can't tell you. Remember? I haven't regained my memory.'

'But I can't leave the Hall yet.' There was a protest in her heart, but Karen knew instinctively that no amount of emotion would make Duncan change his mind. She was aware that he held the whip hand, and unless she did as he wanted then Roy would be in serious trouble. She told herself that an innocent man need have no fear of the law, but it wouldn't be the first time an innocent man was found guilty of some crime he didn't commit.

'You had better be gone by the time I get out of hospital,' Duncan retorted harshly. 'You can always invent some family crisis. My mother is well enough now to do without you. If I come home and find you at the Hall there will be trouble for Roy, and I'll see to it that the most serious charge possible is brought against him.'

'Your own brother!' Karen stared at him with loathing in her eyes. 'How could you do such a dreadful thing?'

'That's none of your business.' He lay back in the bed and closed his eyes. 'You'd better go now. I'm feeling tired. I hope you'll find the sense to do as I want. If you think I don't mean any of it then Roy will suffer, because my memory will return just after I get home.' He lapsed into silence and turned his face away from Karen in dismissal, and she stared at him for a moment.

'I don't think you've judged me correctly, Duncan,' she said at length. 'I wouldn't run out on Roy. If you made such an allegation against him I would have to tell the police about this conversation we've had.'

He opened his eyes and stared up at her, but there was no expression in them. They were dull and lustreless, inanimate, as if he were blind. Then he nodded slowly.

'Your evidence wouldn't be accepted because you would be standing to gain from Roy's innocence,' he said.

'I know a little more about the law

than that!' she retorted.

'Very well, put it to the test. Be at the Hall when I come home and you'll see how far you'll be able to help Roy.' He sneered faintly, and his face took on a repulsive look. Karen moved away from the bed and paused by the door. She looked back at him but his eyes were closed and he was breathing deeply.

Karen sighed, filled with indecision, and she left the hospital and went back to Roy's car. He grinned at her as she got in at his side, and she could not help thinking how dissimilar the two brothers were.

'Well?' he demanded anxiously, and she scrutinized his face for some sign of his guilt. But he seemed only concerned about his brother's state of health. 'How is he?'

'He looks all right,' she said, 'but I believe he's suffering amnesia.'

'So he doesn't remember what happened that afternoon!'

Karen glanced quickly at him, wondering if that fact relieved him, and she felt all her old doubts returning. She pondered over what she should tell him of her visit to Duncan, and knew that he would have to be told something. Duncan asked for her, and he had to have a good reason.

'He seems to think that you were responsible for his injuries that afternoon, Roy!' Her voice was tense, under great strain, and there was a lump in her throat.

'I guessed he would say that.' He stared ahead through the windscreen, and his face was harsh and immobile. There was a trace of bitterness in his tones, and Karen forgot her suspicions and felt only concern for him.

'I don't believe him!' she said firmly. 'You couldn't possibly have done such a thing, Roy.'

'Thanks. It's a relief to know that you believe in me. The trouble is, I can't prove that I wasn't in that area at the time the accident must have happened. I hiked to the cabin, as you know, and the route I took led close to the spot where Duncan lay. I've been convinced since the accident happened that it wasn't purely an accident. There was another man in the area, so the police say, but I'm convinced they don't suspect me. Of course I'm still a possible suspect, but they've partially eliminated me.'

'And if Duncan suddenly regains his memory and says that you are the one who attacked him?'

'I wouldn't put that past him!' He stared as her, noting her apparent distress. 'Is that what he wanted to see you about? Has he put any pressure upon you, Karen?'

'Yes.' She nodded. 'I was going to keep it away from you, Roy, but you have a right to know. Duncan gave me an ultimatum.' She told him slowly what had passed between the two of them, and his face turned angry as he listened.

'That's just the sort of thing Duncan would do,' he said furiously, and his face was white and tense. 'But you don't believe what he's told you, Karen, or you wouldn't have told me. I'm grateful for your trust in me, and I'll tell you what I'm going to do. There's only one way to scotch this little plan of Duncan's and that's by bringing it out into the open. We'll go to see the police now and tell them what Duncan said.'

'I'd rather leave the Hall as Duncan wants, and never see you again, Roy, if it would help,' she told him firmly.

'Then you don't love me!' His gaze was intent as he watched her.

'But I do! I would be willing to go away forever if it would help you!'

'It would be far better if we fought this and remained together, Karen. Isn't that what you want?'

'Yes, Roy,' she said steadily. 'It's all I want.'

He took her hand and squeezed it gently. 'Then let's do something constructive, shall we? Sergeant McKay is investigating this matter, and I trust him. Let's go and see him.'

Karen was afraid, but she knew in her

heart that Roy was right, and she felt that his eagerness to put matters right bespoke of his innocence. She cheered up a little as he drove through the streets of the town and parked outside the police station, but a chill touched her heart as they entered the small red brick building.

It was like a nightmare to wait while Roy explained to the policeman exactly what had happened, and then she had to make a statement of what Duncan had said. Now was the crucial test. If Roy could not prove his innocence then he would face a long term of imprisonment, and Karen knew that fact alone would end all her hopes of love and marriage. But she would lose him if she followed Duncan's wishes and departed from the Hall on some pretext or other. She had nothing to lose by trying to prove Roy's innocence, and everything to gain if she succeeded.

There was no expression on the policeman's face to show what he thought of their story, and Karen's heart almost failed her as she waited his verdict. But he excused himself and left the office. Karen stared at Roy, and she could see by his face that he felt afraid of what might happen next. She reached out and took hold of his hand, squeezing it to reassure him, and he smiled and nodded slowly.

'It will all come right, Karen, you'll see,' he promised.

'I'm sure it will.' She smiled to cover her apprehension, and they waited in what seemed a timeless period of anticipation.

When the sergeant returned, his expression was still strictly impersonal, and he sat down at the desk, apologizing for keeping them waiting. He excused himself again and took up the telephone, and Karen tensed when he called the hospital. He spoke to the switchboard operator, then was put through to the surgeon in charge of Duncan's case. Karen listened stonily, fearing the worst. But the sergeant was asking permission to visit Duncan in order to question him, and the surgeon agreed that a few minutes wouldn't harm the patient.

'I'd like you two to come with me,' Sergeant McKay said as he hung up and got to his feet. 'I presume you came here by car!'

'It's outside,' Roy said.

'Well you can leave it there and travel in the police car with me. I'll bring you back here afterwards to collect it, and there may be some more questions to be asked after I've spoken with your brother.'

'That's all right by me,' Roy said, and Karen was relieved at the sound of so much confidence in his tones.

'Let's go then!' The sergeant led them from the office.

On the way to the hospital again, Karen could not prevent her thoughts from worrying her. As Duncan had told her, no-one would suspect him of lying. If he said he clearly remembered being attacked by Roy then Roy would have a difficult time trying to prove his innocence. Roy himself was beginning to look nervous, and they were silent as they left the car and entered the large building. They walked through the corridors to Duncan's room, and to Karen's mind it seemed as if their steps lagged as they neared it.

The sergeant paused in the corridor and turned to face them. Karen wished he didn't look so foreboding. She could feel her heart thumping, and her legs felt weak. Roy was tense, and she could guess at the thoughts passing through his mind.

'Stay outside,' Sergeant McKay said evenly, 'and don't show yourselves. You can listen at the door, if you wish, to hear what your brother has to say.'

Roy nodded, and Karen took hold of his hand. The policeman stared at them for a moment, then turned away and opened the door of the side ward. He left the door ajar as he crossed to Duncan's bedside, and Karen edged closer, aware that Roy was now gripping her hand very hard. They both heard quite clearly what was said.

'Mr Murray, I'm glad to see you're looking so well now,' McKay said in booming tones. 'I've been waiting some considerable time to talk to you. I understand that your memory isn't quite back to normal yet, or is it?'

'There are some things I cannot remember,' Duncan replied, and his tones were not as strong as when he had spoken to Karen earlier. She trembled when she realized that he was pretending to be weaker than he really was.

'But you can recall what happened to you on the afternoon of your accident,' the policeman prompted.

'I don't know. It's all a bit hazy. I remember taking the dog for a walk.'

'Did you see anyone during that walk?'

'I didn't.'

'Then what happened?'

'The dog was going on ahead. It ran up the slope to the top of the ridge.' Duncan paused, and Karen compressed her lips. Here was where he started lying!

'That's right,' McKay said. 'The dog went to the top of the slope and started a small rock moving on the decline. It bounced in the air just above you, and came down upon your head.'

'How would you know that?' Duncan demanded. 'You seem sure of the facts, Sergeant!'

In the short silence that followed Karen held her breath. She looked into Roy's face, and saw the hope there mingled with fear. Her own hopes were unsteady, rising and falling irrationally. If only Duncan would tell the truth. Then the sergeant spoke again.

'I have managed to find two witnesses to what happened that afternoon, Mr Murray,' he said, 'but I'd rather not say what they told me until I have your story.'

'Two witnesses?' Duncan said with surprise in his voice.

'Two independent witnesses,' the policeman repeated.

'I didn't know there was anyone else around.' Duncan seemed unsure of himself.

'How do you suppose help came to you?' McKay demanded. 'Now, do you recall what happened that afternoon, sir?'

'Yes.' Duncan's voice was suddenly very low and hoarse. 'It happened exactly as you said. The dog went up the slope and dislodged a rock. It tumbled down the slope and I thought it would miss me, but it suddenly struck a projection in the slope and soared up into the air. I didn't have a chance to get out of its way.'

'I see.' McKay's voice grew stronger. 'Then there's no need for me to spend any more time on this case, is there?'

'None at all, Sergeant,' Duncan told him tensely. 'But who were the witnesses?'

'I don't suppose you would know them, but you probably owe your life to them,' McKay said. 'But that will be all, sir. I wish you a speedy recovery, and I hope in future you'll be more careful on the moors.'

'I shall be,' Duncan said, and Karen moved away from the door and turned to face Roy, who was smiling easily.

McKay came out of the room and carefully closed the door at his back. He was smiling now, and there was no sign of his remote manner.

'You heard that, no doubt,' he said.

'We certainly did!' Roy was overjoyed. 'But you didn't mention those witnesses to me, Sergeant. It would have relieved me if I had known about them before, I can tell you.'

'What two witnesses, sir?' McKay met their gazes frankly.

'You mean there were no witnesses?' Karen demanded.

'We have to employ such tactics sometimes,' the policeman said gently. 'If your brother was having trouble remembering exactly what happened then it was up to me to give him what aid I could. From what I had seen at the scene of the accident I deduced what had happened. The dog was responsible, and all we needed was for your brother to corroborate that fact, which he did. Now the case is closed, and you needn't worry about Duncan changing his story in future. If you're ready I'll drive you back to the station for your car.'

'Thank you, but give me one moment,' Roy said eagerly. He turned to Karen and took her into his arms, kissing her soundly in his relief and joy.

Karen glanced over his broad shoulder and saw the policeman smile as he turned away. Then she promptly forgot everything but the fact that she was in Roy's arms, and her heart told her that all her worries were over. Her love knew no bounds and the future beckoned warmly. The pressure of Roy's lips against hers melted the ice of fear that seemed to cling inside her, and she gave herself up to him with no thought that they were standing in a public corridor and were being observed. But this embrace was just a mutual token of what existed between them. Later, she told herself, as Roy drew away, they would find the time and the place to cement their feelings, and suddenly the whole world seemed to change in Karen's sight. Her cares fell away and she seemed to emerge upon a hitherto unknown plane of ecstasy. This was the true state of love, she discovered, and knew that even her rosy expectations would be exceeded.

Other titles in the
Linford Romance Library:

COUNTRY DOCTOR

Phyllis Mallett

After years away, newly qualified Doctor Jane Ashford returns to her hometown in Essex to become a partner in her uncle's practice. Family and friends are delighted to see her again, including Steve Denny, whose crush on her has never faded. But then Jane meets local Doctor Philip Carson, both handsome and lonely; and when his touch kindles a desire that's almost painful in its intensity, she knows he's the right man for her. The problem is, Steve doesn't see it that way — and he intends to make it clear . . .